. . . Cris's viewport was precisely lined up with the creature. It was now rapidly receding into the void above them, but Cris still had plenty of time. Nothing on Earth, native to the planet or otherwise, could outrun a laser beam.

Beams of coherent light shot out of each of Cris's hands and traveled across the gap to the target in a fraction of a millisecond. The lasers cut off automatically a tenth of a second after Cris's mental order to fire, but that was time enough.

Almost instantaneously, the flames coming from the nozzles on the thing's underside were accompanied by two other noticeable bursts of light and fire — explosions where the beams had struck. Before anyone in the capsule could voice a reaction to that, their view of the creature's body was totally obscured by the biggest fireball Cris had ever seen. . . .

D0870623

CYBORG COMMANDO™

BOOK 2

CHASE
INTO
SPACE

by Pamela O'Neill
and Kim Mohan

Cover illustration by Janny Wurts

CHASE INTO SPACE

A CYBORG COMMANDO™ Book

First printing, February 1988
Printed in the United States of America

Distributed to the book trade by the Berkley Publishing Group, 200 Madison Avenue, New York NY 10016

9 8 7 6 5 4 3 2 1

ISBN: 0-441-10294-8

New Infinities Productions, Inc.
P.O. Box 657
Delavan WI 53115

For our friends . . .

Arthur and Lois

. . . who taught us how to be a team.

Prologue

. . . And persevere It did.

Through massive losses and major humiliation.

Through months and months of standing back and watching those infernal man-made monstrosities wreak havoc on Its forces.

It would destroy this planet before It would let this inferior species get away with causing It any more grief.

What did this race think it was doing?

Were its members not aware that It was the Master Race — the Controller of Reality — and that all must bow before It?

That It had the power to create and destroy at will?

That Its ultimate goal was to govern the universe and control all who dwelled within?

That It could keep sending grief to this foolhardy mass of mortality till infinitude?

It could.

But that wasn't part of Its plan.

Trying to ignore the unfamiliar feeling of self-doubt rising inside Itself and struggling to keep a leash on Its barely controlled fury, It planned Its next move.

It would show the arrogant inhabitants of this insignificant planet that It would not stand for the way Its minions had been treated.

There was more than one way to conquer a planet. If the creatures It commanded could not face up to the mechanical creations of humankind, then It would use Its creatures in a different way. Instead of being sent out to ravage far and wide, they would be pulled back around population centers, serving as a noose that would be drawn tighter and tighter around the throat of humankind.

The battle would not be won as quickly, but it would still be won. Soon enough, the artificial warriors that man had created to save himself would have no more reason to exist — because the human race would be extinct.

It had time — much more time than mankind. The Master would have Its revenge. . . .

. . . or so It thought.

1

April 20, 2036

The screams gave it away.

Even if Cyborg Commandos P-17 and C-12 had not already determined the location of their target by electronic means, they would have found it impossible not to get a fix on the bloodcurdling shrieks they had just heard coming from the other side of a building about two hundred yards away.

"Oh, God! We'd better hurry!" Cris Holman, the young man whose brain resided inside P-17's electromechanical body, almost panicked at the sounds he had heard. They had come from human throats, he was sure, but the screams were wild, crazed, almost inhuman. And there were so *many* of them . . .

"Not too fast, kid," said C-12, maintaining his same brisk walking pace. "We can't risk giving ourselves away by going into high gear, and if they've already been caught then there's nothing we can do for those people now." The brain of John Edwards had previously existed inside the body of a professional soldier, and because of that, Commando C-12 was quite a bit cooler than his partner in times of trouble.

Cris fought against letting his emotions get the better of him, as he had done so many times before, and told himself as they continued striding along that their tactics were correct and necessary. They had to advance slowly and methodically to take the monsters by surprise, because they needed that advantage to be sure of killing them. But in the meantime, innocent and helpless people were dying. Although Cris understood why it had to be this way, he still had a hard time accepting it.

Two gunshots punctuated the screams. Then, after a few seconds, silence reigned over the area again. The air was deathly still, and a feeling of dread rose inside Cris as he and John stealthily made their way toward the source of the last sounds they had heard.

Even though he had a good idea what to expect, the carnage Cris saw as he peered around the corner of the building was enough to make him pause and bend over, putting his hands on his knees as though he was trying to keep himself from being sick. Of course, P-17's body could not vomit, but that didn't keep Cris's brain from thinking that he was going to. He let out a soft moan and cursed.

"And you wanted to hurry," John Edwards whispered in a sarcastic but friendly tone, partly to snap Cris out of his distress and partly to cover up the revulsion he was feeling himself. And then, this time sternly, "Come on, kid, get it together!" John moved sideways a couple of steps and crouched down behind a pile of rubble, surveying the scene by peering through an opening in the debris. Cris followed suit, finding his own "window" through the wreckage.

Arrayed in an arc in front of the two Cyborg Commandos and facing away from them were five xenoborgs — the name that military scientists had coined to identify the ghastly, monstrous creatures that had invaded Earth almost a year and a half earlier. They had managed to trap several men and women in a corner where two walls came together and were now in the process of enjoying themselves immensely.

Four of the xenoborgs were fairly small, with bulbous bodies about fourteen feet long and nine or ten feet in diameter at the thickest part. The fifth, obviously a leader type, was about three feet longer and two feet wider than the others. It had one of its tentaclelike appendages wrapped around a laser generator, and it was casually playing the beam back and forth along a strewn-out pile of smoldering human flesh. As it cut the bodies of

11

what used to be about a half-dozen men and women into manageable pieces, the leader and the other four xenoborgs shot out tentacles, grabbed chunks of the flesh and bone, and shoved them into their mouth cavities. To the monsters, it was quite a feast. To Cris Holman and John Edwards, it was one more reason why they had devoted their lives to wiping the xenoborgs from the face of the planet.

Cris was trembling with rage and frustration inside, but he remembered the need for silence and spoke in a low voice. "If we had been just a few minutes earlier, those people—"

"Well, we weren't, and they aren't," John said in a harsh whisper, hoping to get his partner's mind back on the matter at hand. And then, his tone a little softer, he added, "There are only so many of us against hordes of them. We can't save everyone, Cris. You know that."

"Yeah," Cris said coldly. When push came to shove, he was one of the best Cyborg Commandos in the business. P-17 had risked his life willingly many times in the last fourteen months, and had blasted and burned more xenoborgs than he could keep track of. But Cris Holman — the man inside the machine — still couldn't get used to the thought, much less the sight, of humans being destroyed and eaten by the merciless monsters from some other world.

Sometimes he resented John for being so callous about the awful loss of life these creatures were causing, but at the same time he appreciated John's patience with his reactions of sadness and grief. And he had to admit that John's attitude was not only understandable, but probably the correct one for all CCs to have. The problem was that, despite what the logical part of his brain told him, Cris couldn't force his emotional side to think that way all the time.

"What do we do now?" Cris quietly asked his partner, struggling to get control over his emotions. Then he began answering his own question. "You take out the laser, and I'll—"

"No. Not yet. We wait and let those bastard bugs get good and full. Then, just when they're ready for dessert—"

"Do you have to be so disgusting? Those are human beings you're talking about. Humans! Like you and I once were!" Cris had trouble keeping his voice down to a loud whisper.

"Hey! Back off, kid! And I'd rather you didn't remind me of my former physical status. Thinking about my hot-blooded body wasting its precious womanizing years lying around on a bed of ice does nothing to improve my disposition, if you catch my drift."

"Sorry," Cris responded. "I guess I'm just getting discouraged. So many people are dead already, and more and more are dying all the time. We're getting nowhere with these things!"

13

"There's only so much two superhuman mechanical studs like you and yours truly can do. Let's just take 'these things' one at a time," John said, trying to console his partner in his usual half-serious, half-humorous way.

Cris and John had worked together against the alien invaders long enough now to know some very vital bits of information. They knew that these life forms were able to communicate with each other. Many of them, including the leader they were now observing, had some kind of self-contained transmitter that sent out signals to other xenoborgs. By tuning his built-in receiver to the right frequency, any Cyborg Commando could determine the source of a certain xenoborg transmission — which was how Cris and John had been able to locate the group they were about to engage.

They knew that the xenoborgs were brought to earth by enormous creatures that appeared to be part plant, part animal, perhaps even part machine — but their exact nature was not known, since these creatures were heavily armed and no one, not even a CC, had succeeded at getting close to one. They usually landed, dropped off their cargo, and took off again.

And they knew that xenoborgs seemed to get most, if not all, of their nourishment from local life forms, seemingly preferring humans over any other food source. John and Cris, and other CCs, had observed that when xenoborgs were eating, they seemed to become more sluggish and ignorant the longer they continued to feed. Despite this, they were apparently prone to overeating, presumably as a safeguard against not knowing when they would get their next really nourishing meal. One healthy human should have been a full day's sustenance for this entire group of monsters — yet now they were in the process of devouring six people who had ventured out for a reason that would never be known for sure. These monsters would be easy targets, if John and Cris acted at just the right time.

The time was now. The victims were almost entirely consumed. The leader had stopped using its laser, and two of the smaller xenoborgs were feeding slowly instead of ravenously. All of them were still unaware that two concealed CCs were watching their every move.

"Okay, now, how do you want to handle this one, lieutenant?" John asked Cris.

Cris smiled inwardly. He liked being called "lieutenant" — a rank he had earned more than a year ago when he had saved the life of C-12 as well as his own. But he sobered up quickly when one of the smaller creatures began to turn away from its grisly repast and seemed to look in the direction where Cris and John were hidden.

"You take out the laser, and I'll cover you," Cris said, anxious to rid the world of these creatures.

"Here goes," John took a couple of steps backward and then leaped over the ten-foot-high pile of debris in one continuous motion. When he hit the ground, he began running at an angle off to the right, getting himself in position to fire on the tentacle that held the weapon.

At the same time, Cris lunged out from behind his cover, extended his right arm, and began peppering the leader with short laser bursts, designed to distract as much as injure it. The leader, taken by surprise, turned sluggishly to bring its laser to bear on the enemy that was scorching its hindquarters. The movement brought the monster's flank, and the extended weapon, right into John's line of fire.

C-12's first laser shot cut through the tentacle holding the weapon, and the extremity fell to the pavement. Now the monsters were unarmed except for their writhing tentacles and clicking mandibles, and they would never get close enough to John or Cris to make use of those natural attack forms.

The rest was child's play. Without saying a word to each other, John and Cris knew exactly what to do. C-12 turned his laser beam on the two smaller xenoborgs closest to him, and P-17 went to work on the leader.

Cris fired a double burst of lethal light into the bulkiest part of the leader's form, hoping to disable the communication unit imbedded in the monster's body. Amid the sizzling and popping of burning flesh, Cris heard a sparking, crackling sound that told him one of the beams had found the mark. The metallic transmitter was ruined, which meant that any other monsters in the area would no longer be able to zero in on where their comrades were being slaughtered.

The next order of business was to cut the leader's legs out from under it, just as John had already done with the two beasts he had attacked. With one sweep of his laser across the lower portion of the thing's bulk, Cris chopped off three of the spindly legs that supported the massive body. Now three of the five xenoborgs were stationary, their remaining legs scrambling frantically in a futile attempt to move their bodies away from the killing blasts.

Meanwhile, the other two xenoborgs couldn't go anywhere; they were trapped against the same two walls where the unfortunate humans had been cornered just a few minutes earlier. One of them, using what little intelligence it apparently had, tried to take cover behind the wounded, smoldering body of its leader. Cris took great pleasure in training another double laser burst on the leader's body. The beams practically chopped the thing in half from top to bottom — and as they came out the other side of its body, they also made two searing incisions in the xenoborg that was trying to hide.

Rather than try to run or fight, the fifth xenoborg

simply dropped in its tracks. Its legs disappeared beneath its sagging underbelly, and its extremities flopped haphazardly to the ground. Cris had seen this maneuver before, and he wasn't sure if the monster was trying to play dead or trying to appear willing to surrender. Either way, it made no difference; he knew from experience that if he approached the creature and tried to take it prisoner, its tentacles and mandibles would suddenly come back to life in one final effort to kill or be killed. He had been fooled once, and nearly had his left arm torn off as a result. He would not be fooled again.

While C-12 started to chop and scorch the wounded xenoborgs into smaller chunks, Cris strolled over to within ten feet of the "dead" monster's motionless tentacles. He thought he could almost sense the thing expecting him to step closer. Instead, he stopped and raised his right arm until it was parallel to the ground.

"I hope you enjoyed your last meal, you ugly bastard!" Cris shouted. He activated his laser again, this time in a single beam that he tracked slowly across the creature's body from left to right. The thing abandoned its pretense and began flailing its tentacles in the air, to no avail. Then Cris bounded to one side and fired again, separating the creature's front part from the rest of its body. He cut three more diagonal swaths across its body, effectively carving the xenoborg into about a dozen different pieces. He would have loved to keep slicing until the thing was reduced to an amorphous pile of jelly, but he knew that would be an unnecessary and foolish waste of power.

Cris stepped back to where he could see C-12 standing a few yards away. John raised the knuckles of his right hand to his face and seemed to blow across them in a parody of a nineteenth-century gunfighter. Then he saluted in P-17's direction and called out, "Ready for phase two?"

"Let's cook 'em," Cris said exuberantly. Standing just a few paces away from the chunks of monster flesh that were still pulsing and twitching, both CCs pointed the palms of their hands toward the unearthly mess and turned on their microwave projectors. Within seconds, the entire surface of the pulpy globs began to sizzle and pop. The large cells that made up each xenoborg's body burst, and the moisture inside each one either boiled away or trickled in rivulets along cracks in the pavement.

The "cooking" was necessary because xenoborgs didn't die the way humans did. As long as even a small group of cells remained undestroyed, the monsters could generate new cells and regrow. This didn't always happen, but there was no sense in taking chances. It was best to use the microwave projectors at point-blank range, because it took a much greater amount of power to operate them at a longer distance. That was why Cris and John used their lasers first, to disable and immobilize the monsters so they could get as close as possible before using what John described as "phase two."

In a short time all that remained of the xenoborgs were assorted shapeless piles of withered, blistered flesh. Five more creatures would never kill again.

"I guess they're well done," Cris said with satisfaction as he lowered his arms and swept his gaze across the scene. His eye caught sight of some of the visible human remains near the wall, and he stood motionless and silent for a moment.

John noticed what was happening and again tried to get Cris's mind off the tragic aspect of what they had just been through. "You sure have come a long way since the first time you fried one of these suckers!" he said, a hint of mischief in his tone.

"Did you have to bring that up again?" Cris asked, turning toward his companion.

John began walking slowly away from the combat scene. As Cris fell into step beside him, he pursued the subject, pretending to be offended. "I was just trying to be complimentary—"

"That'll be the day!"

"—but I must admit you did look pretty hysterical with that monster goo all over you!" The first time Cris had used his microwave projectors was also the first time he and John had gone on a mission together. Not knowing any better at the time, Cris had used the beams at their highest intensity against a target at close range. The result was a squishy explosion of superheated xenoborg flesh that had coated Cris, and everything else in a twenty-foot radius, with the remains.

"I don't need you to remind me, pal," Cris said, putting heavy emphasis on the last word. "It took a long time for my olfactory sensors to recover. For weeks afterward, every time I turned my sniffer back on I caught a whiff of dead monster flesh. Sometimes I think I can still smell that awful stuff!"

"I'll bet the sanitation workers who had to clean you up back at the base needed nose transplants afterward. You smelled worse than a hundred dead skunks!"

"Yeah, well, everybody makes mistakes," said Cris, a little edgily.

"Sorry," said John with a combination of sincerity and gentle sarcasm. "I shouldn't be teasing you about something so trivial that happened so long ago."

"No, you shouldn't, but you seem to like doing it anyway," Cris said skeptically.

"I'm not going to bring up that little episode ever again. I swear," John said overdramatically.

"Fine. Let's drop it."

"Okay. I'll be happy to drop it." Then, almost without missing a beat, he added, "But here's something that didn't happen so long ago. Remember that little episode last week when you tried to tighten your elbow plate and almost put a hole in your arm? Didn't anyone ever teach you how to screw, boy?"

"Okay, C-12, you've had it!" Cris said, pointing his little finger at John and making a fake lunge in his direction.

"Ah, I just love a good street fight. But most of us ganglords use knives, not drills," John said with mock seriousness.

"Damn! I can never remember which finger's which!" Cris said pitifully, quickly retracting the drill and lowering his arm.

John laughed uproariously over his partner's consternation. A few days ago while they were relaxing together, Cris noticed a loose screw in the armor plate covering his left elbow. Instead of extending his right index finger, which contained a retractable screwdriver blade, he stuck out his little finger — the digit containing a small, high-speed drill — and came within an inch or so of making matters worse instead of better. He was forever confusing one finger with the other when it came to using his built-in tools.

Cris tried to ignore his friend's laughter, at the same time silently resolving never to make that mistake again. "Go ahead. Have your fun. I can take it. Since my operation I have pretty broad shoulders, you know."

"I'll tell you, kid," John said, regaining his composure, "being your partner is more fun than wrestling an army of xenoborgs — and probably twice as hazardous."

"Oh, yeah? Well, who was it that saved your life, huh? I should have left you up on that rooftop when I had the chance and let those creatures blow you to bits, you ungrateful pig!"

John sobered quickly. "We *were* lucky that day, weren't we?"

"Lucky!?" Cris shouted angrily. "You call what I did *lucky*? I'd say you'll be lucky to get to accompany me back to base — if you can keep up with me!" And with that Cris threw his cybernetic frame into ultraspeed mode and took off, his arms and legs a blur as he sprinted down the middle of the deserted street.

"Hey, you P-brain! I'll get you for this!" By the time John could utter that statement and engage ultraspeed himself, P-17 was almost out of sight in the distance. Two minutes and five miles later, just outside one of the access bays leading down to the CCF Primary Base in Manitowoc, Wisconsin, Cris finally came to a stop. John pulled up beside him a couple of seconds later, and the two of them entered the complex together, cursing each other in comradely fashion. The technicians who met them inside barely took note of their boisterous entrance, since they had long since become accustomed to the way these two super-soldiers acted when they were teamed together.

John and Cris fed brief reports about their mission into the base's data banks, said their good-nights, and each headed in the direction of his private quarters. Their shift was over for today, and another pair of CCs had already left the complex to take their place outside.

Cris inserted the index finger of his left hand into the security lock outside his quarters. A panel in the wall slid aside to allow him passage. Once he was inside, the door closed neatly and quietly behind him. He walked over to a pair of sockets on the floor and slipped his feet inside the housings. He felt the electrical power flow into and through his body, and after several minutes an indicator light on the power sockets went on to tell him that his primary battery was fully recharged.

Although his mechanical body never felt fatigue, Cris Holman was mentally tired. And he was looking forward to shutting down for the day.

It had been a long fourteen months, yet in some ways it seemed like only yesterday since the xenoborgs had come to Earth and annihilated at least one-third of its human population, including his father, his stepmother, his little sister, and the woman he had intended to marry. "Oh, Maura," Cris said with a loud sigh. "I doubt I'll ever be able to get you off my mind." He walked over and turned on his videocommunicator. A message was waiting for him, and the face of the messenger made him smile inside. Then he noticed his mother's somber expression, and his own mood darkened abruptly.

"P-17 and C-12, I've been asked to inform you that the two of you are wanted in the main briefing room as soon as possible after you get back and recharge. Please hurry." Most of Nora Whitaker's message was delivered in a flat, businesslike tone — but the two words she added at the end were obviously not part of what she was supposed to say, and she seemed on the verge of tears as she said them.

The screen went blank, but Cris stared at it for another couple of seconds and wondered what it was, other than the usual state of affairs, that seemed to be worrying his mother. Then he headed for the door.

John and Cris almost ran head-on into each other as they were heading toward each other's quarters.

"She sounded a little too shook up to suit me," John said.

"I know. Do you think maybe she's—"

"Nah. She hasn't had — or wanted — a drink in a long time," John interrupted before Cris could finish the question.

"Well, she does worry about us when we're in the field. Maybe the tension has finally gotten to her."

"Cris, I've known your mother for a long time now — longer than you have — and I can tell that what you saw on your screen just now was not alcohol-induced. But she does seem worried about

25

something out of the ordinary, and that was an urgent message. We better get going instead of standing here speculating," John said. He turned and headed back the way he had come, toward the briefing room.

"Okay," said Cris, following John down the narrow corridor. He was sure of his abilities and eager for a new challenge — assuming that was what the urgency was about. But he was just as anxious, in a negative way, about the mood his mother had projected. He tried to imagine what could have happened since he and John had left on their mission. As he soon found out, nothing that occurred to him was even remotely close to the truth.

Of course it wasn't. How could they have possibly known what the Master had in store for them? They were only human — inferior life forms. It was something they would never understand.

2

April 20, 2036

The main briefing room was deceptively small for its name — somewhat larger than the cubicles where individual CCs or two-unit teams usually went to get instructions before missions, but much smaller than the auditorium area where practically all of the base's personnel could be comfortably gathered at one time. When Cris and John entered, the room contained two people.

Nora Whitaker was seated in a chair at the back of the room; on the wall opposite her was a large video screen. Sitting at a small table against one side wall was a civilian man in a white lab coat. Cris was certain he had never seen the man before. A chair next to the man was vacant.

The instant that John came through the door, with Cris on his heels, Nora pushed a button on the portable videocom in her lap and said in a subdued tone of voice, "They're here, sir." John and Cris went directly to where she was seated, but couldn't get there in time to get a glimpse of the screen before it went blank. Nora put on a smile for them as they approached, but the expression was obviously forced.

"Hi, mom," Cris said cheerily, reaching out and briefly touching her shoulder. Nora returned his greeting with a warm smile. Cris immediately took note of the worried, tired look in her eyes.

"What's up?" John asked over Cris's words, saying it as a form of greeting but also meaning it as a deliberate question. "Who's that?" he added, pointing his thumb back over his shoulder toward the man, who was sitting silently, trying to look busy as he scanned some papers in front of him.

"Any questions you may have will be answered shortly. For now, please take seats over there, facing the table, and wait until the general arrives." Nora said, her tone not quite as official as her words, but what she said made it clear that Nora was not able, or authorized, to answer any questions. She looked into Cris's face, then John's, trying to express with her eyes what she could not utter with her lips. Both of them knew better than to press her for more information under the circumstances, so they silently complied.

Cris knew "the general" could only be Gen. Ernest Garrison, the hard-bitten career soldier who was in charge of military operations at the Manitowoc base. It was common knowledge that no Cyborg Commando mission ever took place without the general's explicit or implicit consent; he was the one man who knew the status and the whereabouts of every CC at all times. But Cris had never heard of an occasion when the general himself attended or delivered a mission briefing. By the time the man strode into the room a minute and a half later, Cris was so full of anxiety he could barely control himself.

Everyone in the room rose when he entered. "Sit, sit," he said gruffly as he moved behind the table and took the empty seat. Without acknowledging any of those present individually, he stared straight ahead at P-17 and C-12 and began to speak.

"What I am about to say is being disseminated on a need-to-know basis. You will share none of it with anyone. You will not discuss it with anyone other than those who are presently in this room with you, and you will not often have occasion to do even that."

The general paused, as if waiting for an acknowledgment or response. Cris decided he would follow John's lead; if C-12 said "Yessir" or anything else, he would chime right in. John remained silent, impassive, looking straight ahead, so Cris did the same. He cast a slight sideways glance in Nora's direction (which he could do, of course, without moving his eyes) and found her also sitting stock still, face and eyes rigidly forward. She doesn't need to sit at attention, thought Cris. Why isn't she looking at us? At me?

A few seconds later the general took a deep breath and got right down to business.

"We are winning a lot of battles, gentlemen. But we are losing the war." At this, Nora cleared her throat softly and brought one hand up under her chin, as if she needed to support it. She looked distraught to Cris, but at the same time he got the impression that she had already heard this news; she did not seem shocked or even the least bit surprised.

"Accumulated reports from our bases around the world indicate that, on the average, each member of the Cyborg Commando Force destroys about sixty-five xenoborgs in a four-month period before he or she is killed or disabled. In a normal war, that would be an excellent kill ratio — but I hardly need to tell you that this is not a normal war.

"The worldwide xenoborg population is estimated to be six hundred thousand. As of today, there are slightly less than one thousand functional Cyborg Commando units. Approximately twenty new ones are being created every week — only slightly more than the number that are disabled or destroyed in the same length of time.

"Mixed into this formula is the fact that every week, many thousands of human beings are dying in xenoborg assaults, and a few thousand more from disease, starvation, or some other indirect cause precipitated by the invasion.

"If the number of active Cyborg Commandos remains essentially constant, as it has for the last few months, and the number of xenoborgs is not augmented by . . . new arrivals, it will be at least another three years before the invaders are exterminated. By then it may be too late."

The general paused briefly to let his words sink in. Then, as though he didn't trust those present to be able to understand the significance of what he had just said, he restated his last remark in a different fashion. "I'll dispense with the hard numbers at this point, gentlemen. Suffice it to say that if it takes that long, even if we succeed, there won't be enough left of this planet, or its people, to make the reward worth the effort."

General Garrison leaned back in his seat — not because he was done, but because he had to take a bit of a break before continuing. "And now, the bottom line."

As the general leaned forward again and rested his elbows on the table, Cris stiffened in his seat. He felt John do the same thing. He saw Nora grip the arms of her chair, a gesture that couldn't conceal her trembling. Even if she has heard this before, Cris thought, I guess it isn't any easier to take the second time. Instead of worrying about what the general's information meant for him, he thought about his mother and the rest of the human race. Given the skills of his body and his brain, a certain amount of luck, and a dependable source of power for recharging, P-17 could live for a long, long time. But what would there be to live for if . . . ?

"The only way we can hope to win, and win soon enough for the victory to be significant, is to bring thousands of new men and women into the Cyborg Commando program. Each of you in this room will have a vital role in indirectly helping that event to occur."

The general motioned toward the man on his right. "Gentlemen, this is Doctor Francis Higgins. He has been brought here from our Command base in New Orleans, at great risk to himself and the ones who helped transport him. His specialty is neurobiology; in fact, he is the foremost authority in that field left alive on the North American continent.

"The individual seated to your right," he added, nodding toward Nora, "hardly needs to be introduced. Doctor Whitaker has more seniority than any other scientist in the Cyborg Commando program, and because of the length of her tenure and the depth of her experience has a wider range of knowledge about all aspects of the program than any other person on this half of the planet. I am well aware that the two of you in this room know her on a more personal level. That does not concern me.

"Beginning immediately, Doctors Higgins and

Whitaker will lead a team of scientists and technicians charged with finally ascertaining how to reverse the cybernetic implantation procedure — how to take the living brain out of a Cyborg Commando and put it back in the body it was originally taken out of."

"No shit?" John blurted out, forgetting for the moment whom it was that he was addressing in such crude form.

"None at all, John." Nora spoke up before the general had a chance to verbally reprimand the soldier. She flashed an encouraging smile in Cris's direction. The two cyborgs could barely contain their elation. But Nora's sudden smile just as suddenly gave way to the somber expression she had previously displayed, and she quickly added, "That's the good news. But there is more, and it's far from pleasant." Cris, who had been about to jump up and rush to give his mother a hug, was held back by the warning signals in his mother's eyes.

"If you are through, Doctor Whitaker, I will continue." The general flashed a stern look in Nora's direction and went on. "This is obviously cheery news for those who have already undergone the transplant. But more importantly, the breakthrough — when it comes — will enable us to recruit many more Cyborg Commando candidates. The main reason our numbers have remained so low is that most qualified people don't want to risk giving up their humanity, even to help save their own lives."

Cris thought he detected a tinge of disgust in the general's voice at that point. It was rumored around the base that General Garrison was strongly in favor of forcing every candidate to go through with the transplant. However, the scientists had proven that drafting people into the CC service would be a waste of time and effort. Everyone at the base had heard the horror stories about candidates who had changed their minds after going through the transplant operation. Most of those went quietly crazy; others, not so quietly. It was clear, judging from these incidents, that if the operation was ever performed on a candidate who was unwilling or even uncertain, the outcome would be no better.

"Once we can guarantee people that they can become human again — and prove it to them by documenting several successful reversals — the Cyborg Commando Force will greatly multiply in number, and our chances of beating back this invasion in time will improve accordingly."

The general leaned back in his chair again, and Cris correctly guessed that this was a prelude to another change of subject — but the man's next words took Cris completely by surprise.

"To be honest, I don't expect either one of you to ever have to undergo a brain transplant reversal procedure, no matter how commonplace that operation becomes — because, gentlemen, I wouldn't give either one of you good odds for living through the missions I am about to assign you." General Garrison said the words in a tone devoid of emotion, his eyes dark beneath a furrowed brow. Nora gasped, obviously not expecting to hear that prediction.

"You told me the missions were dangerous, general. You never said anything about impossible!" Nora blurted out, leaning forward in her seat and glaring angrily at her superior.

"The tasks are not impossible, doctor. But they are very dangerous, and, even if these two accomplish what they are sent to do, there is a better chance they will die in the process than there is that they will return intact." The general was beginning to regret having agreed to allow the woman to be present for the briefing. She may be a top professional, but she was also a mother, and he kept forgetting the emotional side of the human race. These days all that mattered to him was helping to ensure its survival.

"Then why send them? Why not send two others?" Nora asked, almost frantically.

"Because, despite their eccentricities and their tendency toward foolishness, units C-12 and P-17 are by far the most successful units in this sector of the CCF." He directed the rest of his answer toward Cris and John. "Because of that, you are about to receive orders for missions that are far more dangerous than anything you have been required to do before. And for that reason, I want both of you to realize that everything possible is being done to insure that if you don't get back, your sacrifices will not have been in vain."

"How comforting."

The sarcastic remark came from John, who found it impossible to simply sit and listen any longer.

The general seemed to ignore the interruption. "When this briefing is over, you will receive separate instructions for missions that are crucial to the success of the Cyborg Commando program. Even as accomplished as both of you are, there is a good possibility that the tasks we require of you will be . . . unattainable. But if we didn't send out the best we've got, there probably wouldn't be any chance of success at all."

"So this is what we get for being good at what we do," snapped John. "Suicide missions, huh?"

"At least send us out together," said Cris forcefully. Out of the corner of his eye, he saw his mother shake her head slowly and bite her lip, trying to keep from breaking down.

This time General Garrison responded to their remarks. "Yes, C-12, this is what you get. You get a chance to do something of extreme difficulty and indescribable importance — because you have proven yourselves capable of undertaking tasks of this magnitude. For anyone else, these would quite possibly be suicide missions — and we could find others willing to undertake them — but the two of you at least have a chance, however small, of both succeeding and surviving.

"And no, you can't go out together, for two good reasons. First of all, both of these jobs have to be undertaken at the same time — right now. And even if one of them could wait, we wouldn't risk both of you on one of these missions anyway.

"I think that about wraps it up. You have a choice to make here, gentlemen. No one will force you to accept these assignments. However, be aware of the fact that if something drastic is not done soon, there won't be much point in continuing this losing battle. You will be given further details in your individual briefing sessions, after which you will each have an hour to make up your mind. If you reject these assignments, you will carry on the way you've been without interruption and we will not speak of this again. If you decide to accept them, and we hope to God you do, then you will each be given two days to receive and absorb your instructions. You will leave immediately thereafter. Gentlemen, I wish you luck. And I commend you in advance for your courage." And with that General Garrison rose and left the room. Doctor Higgins followed.

John Edwards stood up, turned, and spat out a curse as he drove his fist through the wall behind his chair. At the same time, Cris was up and moving toward his mother. By the time he reached the side of her chair, she was sobbing. She knew even before they did which choices her son and John would make. Of course they would go out. But would they get back? That was what she didn't know, and that was why she cried.

Before It — the Master — was finished with this conquest, more than a few tears would be shed. The lucky ones would be those who didn't live long enough to cry over their fate.

3

April 21, 2036

"I should have known," Cris said warmly as he extended his hand. "Hello, Traynor."

"Good to see you again, P-17," the other man responded. "Why do you think you 'should have known'?"

"It figures. You were the one who briefed me for my first mission. It's only fitting that you be the one who briefs me for my last, don't you think?"

That first briefing had been more than a year ago, just before P-17's first excursion into the outside world. Traynor had been responsible for getting Cris Holman's brain acclimated to its new electromechanical body, and had followed P-17's progress up to and through his first mission in the field. Then the man had all but disappeared from Cris's life; he had other new CCs to train, and P-17 had taken to his new life so quickly and readily that he had needed virtually no followup instructions or supervision. Traynor and P-17 saw each other occasionally and had kept up superficially with what each was doing, but they hadn't had any official, professional contact for a long time.

"Well," Traynor said, "nobody told me *why* I got this assignment. They just gave me instructions, and I'm carrying them out. But there's one thing I do know. Your present attitude is going to make preparing you for this task as hard as it was teaching you to manipulate a lock over a year ago." The man smiled warmly, but his words had the desired impact.

Traynor had taught Cris some valuable lessons, perhaps the most useful one being that nothing is acccomplished when frustration and anger are allowed to get in the way. Cris smiled inwardly, trying to recall just how many times Traynor had obliged him to try manipulating a combination lock with his new, still-clumsy cybernetic fingers before he actually accomplished the task. And then how many times had he made him repeat the procedure before he was convinced that the new soldier could perform the same task over and over again on command. "So why aren't you busy whipping one of the new recruits into shape? That is what you enjoy most in life, isn't it?" Cris delivered the question in a friendly, teasing tone of voice.

Traynor smiled. "I'm happy to see you still have a sense of humor, such as it is. But to answer your first question, for some time now I've been in charge of briefing CCs who are about to be sent out on high-risk missions. This is your lucky day, P-17."

Traynor had become very good at imparting information and getting the facts across while at the same time boosting the morale of the soldiers he was instructing. He certainly had a much better "deskside manner" than someone like General Garrison, and that was especially important when it came to dealing with CCs, such as Cris, who had not been members of the military before their transplants. So, Cris's crudely worded assumption had been essentially correct. But Traynor was not about to confirm that; his job was to build confidence, not erode it.

"Okay, doc," Cris said. "I guess it doesn't matter. Just tell me what I'm supposed to do."

At that moment the door to the small briefing room opened and another Cyborg Commando walked into the room. "Hello, S-24," said Traynor. "Now that you're here, we can get started."

Cris had worked with a lot of different CCs before, but he had never been on a mission with one of the new "S" models. Externally the other CC was technologically identical to him — all the same stuff in all the same places — but the body from the neck to the waist was much thinner than P-17's. The chest cavity was scarcely larger than it needed to be to contain the capsule in which S-

41

24's organic brain was housed. Protruding from the undersized shoulders were two arms that looked spindly and gangly. The head was normal-sized, or almost so, but looked grossly large perched atop the nearly cylindrical torso. The hips, legs, and feet were also roughly the same size and length as those of P-17, but again they looked out of place connected to the compact upper body.

"Is this my—"

Traynor didn't let Cris finish the question. "Corporal S-24, this is Lieutenant P-17. He'll be your superior for this assignment." S-24 nodded toward Cris, saluted, and held out his right hand.

"Hello . . . corporal," Cris said, irritated at himself for letting the words come out in such an uncertain tone. He returned the salute and then took S-24's hand briefly, gingerly, the way an adult man would shake hands with an eight-year-old child. Cris was surprised and more than a little annoyed when the other CC did not speak, but instead simply took a seat beside Cris and turned his attention to Traynor.

Cris was immediately put off by S-24's refusal to return the verbal greeting and also a little annoyed that the impropriety didn't seem to bother Traynor, who was smiling politely at both of them. I am pretty well known around here, thought Cris. Even if I didn't outrank him, I would deserve at least a "hello" from this rookie.

Who does this guy think he is, anyway? Cris

asked silently, stopping just short of voicing the question to Traynor. The man's next remark unsettled Cris a bit, because he could imagine Traynor answering the question in eactly that way. . . .

"You'll have a little time to get to know each other later," said Traynor, again letting a small grin cross his face as he looked first at P-17 and then at S-24. "Right now we have to get down to business. And the business is this: We have more problems than merely a few hundred thousand xenoborgs."

"What do you mean?" Cris blurted out. "Are there more bugs coming down?"

"No, we don't think so. We've recorded some landings of the creatures they use for transportation, but we've also seen some of these ships take off with full loads. Apparently they're moving . . . troops . . . around, reinforcing places where we've hit them hard and leaving only token forces in areas they've already secured.

"That's not our problem — or, at least, not your problem. There is another type of alien creature on this planet, far less numerous than the xenoborgs but posing much more of a threat. We don't know much about them yet, but they seem to be a variation of the vessels used to transport the xenoborgs — the things we call teleborgs.

"But these teleborgs are stationary. Once they land, they stay put, and they grow — some of them are as much as two hundred feet in diameter. They have non-natural attack and defense capabilities, just as many of the xenoborgs do, only on a much larger scale.

"The largest ones, in particular, are practically impervious to any kind of direct attack we've been able to mount. They can shoot most planes and missiles out of the air before we get even close to firing on them — and we don't have enough airborne weapons to keep sending out dozens of them at a time in the hope that a few will get through. We've tried high-altitude bombers, which are pretty successful at getting through a teleborg's defense network and getting in range, but most of the bombs that are dropped impact away from the target, and a lot of those that do come down on the money are hit and detonated in mid-air before they can do any damage."

"Why not try a ground assault?" Cris asked. "A squad of ten of us should be able to surround the thing and blast it to bits."

"Possibly," Traynor said, "except for two factors I haven't told you about yet. First, every one of these things we've located so far has been stationed in an area of extremely dense cover — forests, jungles, cities. You can't hit it at long range from ground level. The immediate area around each teleborg is barren and devastated, apparently because they assimilate any nearby organic matter for nourishment. But by the time you could get close enough for a clean shot at one, it would also be able to draw a bead on you — and judging by what they've done to our jet fighters and missiles, you don't want that to happen.

"Second, each one of these things apparently serves as a headquarters or a gathering spot for xenoborgs — so in order to attack one of them, you'd also have to fight your way in, and back out again, through a swarm of bugs thicker than you've ever had to deal with before. Even if you and the rest of a CC squad could accomplish that — which I doubt — you'd have nowhere to recharge along the way, and a whole lot of trouble getting back to a place of safety before your primaries went dead."

Cric was not at all pleased by any of what he had heard, and the words "suicide mission," in John's voice, came into his mind. But he fought back his pessimism by reminding himself that he still hadn't been told what he and his new partner were supposed to do.

"You're painting an awfully dark picture, doc," he said to Traynor. "What I need to hear from you right now is that there's a ray of light in the middle of all this murkiness."

"Indeed there is, P-17. You and S-24 are going to help us destroy a teleborg. If the plan works once, it can be made to work over and over. We can kill a lot of teleborgs — and, not incidentally, demonstrate to all those uncertain, potential CCs out there that becoming a Cyborg Commando *is* a big contribution to the survival of the human race.

Too many people have become discouraged because the world is so overwhelmed with xenoborgs, not to mention the teleborgs that are planted here and there. They don't think that their 'sacrifice' would make any difference, but if we can show them that a CC can accomplish something of this magnitude—"

"I know what you're saying," Cris interrupted. "This is sort of a combination combat mission and public-relations stunt, right?" He didn't wait for that question to be answered. "Okay, I'm in. But just how do you propose to pull this off?"

Traynor paused before answering. Then slowly, his eyes twinkling mischievously, he replied with obvious pleasure. "We're going to start by giving it exactly what it wants."

* * *

Fifteen minutes later, Traynor had finished explaining the meaning of that remark. Cris was relaxed, confident, almost buoyant. As for S-24 . . . well, it was hard to tell what he thought or felt. The corporal had remained motionless and silent throughout the entire briefing. But that didn't deflate Cris's spirits at all. If I have to, he thought, I can pull this off all by myself.

"It's a good plan," Cris said to Traynor.

"Good? Is that the best you can do?" Traynor's eyes were wide, his expression incredulous. "I'll have you know it took six colonels two weeks to come up with the idea." Cris almost believed that for a second, until Traynor's face broke into a wide smile. The man laughed and added, "Okay. Would you believe two technicians and, at most, forty-five minutes?"

"I would," said Cris, "as long as you weren't one of the technicians."

Traynor frowned, drew back as though he had been stung, and then smiled again. "If your mind is as sharp as your tongue, I'd say you have an excellent chance of making this work."

"Excellent at least. No offense to the uncommunicative corporal here, but this sounds like a one-man job to me."

"And no offense to you, P-17, but there's something you don't completely understand yet."

"Such as?"

"Such as, how are you going to squeeze those manly shoulders through a passageway that's no more than two feet in diameter?"

"Uhhh . . ."

"Just what I thought you'd say. Remember the plan: You're the firepower and the insurance, S-24 is the infiltrator."

"Okay, but how is he going to get the *lower* part of his body through? Some kind crash diet?"

"Good guess," Traynor said. "Show him, S-24."

Cris heard a pair of clicks that seemed to come from the seat of the corporal's chair. Then S-24 bent his elbows and pulled his arms back until he could grasp the sides of his chair with his hands. He slowly straightened his arms until his elbows were locked, which raised his torso up out of the seat of the chair . . .

. . . and his legs stayed where they were!

"What the . . ." Cris jumped out of his chair, whirled, and knelt down in front of the CC, waving his hand back and forth across the space between the torso and the hips. "How did you *do* that?"

Then S-24 spoke, in a voice that Cris Holman knew almost as well as his own.

"No problem. The latest thing in CC technology — interchangeable buns."

"Oh, God," Cris whispered. "Tony? Is that you, Tony?"

"Yeah, Cris. It's me."

P-17 threw out his arms, then stopped in mid-lunge while S-24 lowered his torso and reconnected the parts of his body. The two Cyborg Commandos embraced, and in the background Traynor beamed with happiness and pride.

Cris Holman and Tony Minelli, who had risked their lives together in human bodies, were about to do the same thing in artificial ones. But there was nothing artificial about the bond between them.

"We're going to be one hell of a team," Cris said when the moment of silence had passed.

"For sure," said Tony, looking down into his lap. "All three of us."

4

April 21, 2036

John knew he had heard right, but he was not at all prepared for what his audio receptors had just tuned in on. And he was not in the mood. . . . "You want me to track down a malfunctioning cyborg, render him powerless, and bring him back to base?" he asked incredulously.

"It."

"Excuse me?" John asked.

"It. You said 'him,' and what you're after is the machine. The human inside the apparatus is either no longer functional or temporarily out of synch. Either way, what we have running around wild out there is not a 'him,'" Major Loren Williams said, his expression never changing from its fixed scowl.

"And you have no idea where he — ah, 'it' — is?"

"Of course we know — it's somewhere in this area. We just don't know exactly where at the moment. We get readings on it sporadically," the major said. Then he added, somewhat passionately, "The damn thing keeps moving around on us. And its tracking device is all screwed up."

"So how in the hell am I supposed to be able to locate 'it'?" John again emphasized that last word, almost as though he was trying to irritate the major. Trying or not, he succeeded.

"Look, you have your orders, lieutenant! How you go about carrying them out is up to you—"

"I haven't decided yet *if* I'm going to carry them out, major . . . sir!" John interrupted angrily.

"Why not try using some of that massive brain power you so-called super-soldiers are supposed to have?" The major's face was a bright red now, but his look was one of regret for having lost control. And John took advantage of the mood.

"In the first place, *Major* Williams," he said, placing heavy emphasis on the man's title, "in spite of your obvious rank, I am not just some flunkie you can kick around. In the second place, I'm not about to undertake a mission until all of my questions are answered, whether the orders come from you or the head of the Trans-American Union. And in the third place" — John's tone was becoming increasingly louder and angrier with every word — "I've never had *anything* handed to me. I paid dearly for the dubious honor of defending this planet and the likes of you from those big bad bugs we're fighting out there. So I suggest you do something about whatever bugs you have up your fat—"

"May I remind you, Lieutenant Edwards," the now-enraged major interrupted, his face a brilliant shade of crimson, and almost all of his three hundred pounds of flabby flesh shaking uncontrollably, "that you are a member of the United States armed forces, of which you are still, super circuitry or not, a lower-ranking member than yours truly. And if you ever address me in this manner again I will have no choice but to—"

"What? What are you going to do, major? Take away my batteries? Repossess my microwave and make me go back to slow cooking? Sit on me until I break?"

John's last insult caused the major to lose any semblance of rationality. Williams nearly screamed the first part of his response. "All right, lieutenant, we'll play it your way. You are hereby confined to your quarters until further notice. As of this moment you are no longer considered an operative member of the Cyborg Commando Force."

"About time I got a vacation!" John said, in spite of the fact that he knew he was digging himself in deeper.

"You're dismissed, Mister Edwards." The major took obvious pleasure in addressing his tormentor by a civilian title. John winced inwardly. He left the room without another word.

"Shit!" he cursed as soon as the door of his room had slid in place behind him. "What the hell possessed me to act like that?" He asked himself aloud as he let his body drop loosely into one of the steel-framed chairs in his quarters. He didn't physically need the rest, and in his present state he never would. But the familiar physical act did much for his tired mental state. He had almost succeeded in dozing off when his videocommunicator began bleeping insistently. "Oh, go away," John said sluggishly, not bothering to turn it on. The noise continued and he finally got up and walked over to the set, cursing all the way. "This better be good," he said as he switched on the unit.

"John, what's going on?" Nora's worried face stared at him from the screen.

He tapped a message out on the keys, purposely not turning on the video sender or audio transmitters that would have allowed her to see his face or hear his voice.

"I was trying to get some sleep, that's what's going on! Can't a former person get any rest around here? Even machines need to shut down once in a while!"

There was a pause while the message was sent and then Nora's face reappeared on the screen, this time wearing a combined look of sympathy and understanding. When she spoke it was in a soft, compassionate tone. "Come see me, John. I'd be happy to listen."

John paused and then slowly tapped out a message on the keyboard. "I think I'd like that, but you'll have to come here, if you don't mind. Daddy grounded me."

A few minutes later Nora pressed the buzzer indicating her presence outside John's door. The barrier quickly slid aside, allowing her passage into the room.

John Edwards and Nora Whitaker had known each other since the early days of the Cyborg Commando program, long before the first xenoborgs appeared in the sky above an unsuspecting planet. Nora had been a high-ranking civilian staff member since the virtual inception of the program, and John had volunteered for one of the earliest brain transplant operations nearly five years ago.

The two became friends before his brain was installed in the cybernetic body designated C-12. Then they went their separate ways and kept up on what each other was doing through official channels, but weren't reunited until shortly after the invasion, when they both ended up working out of the base at Manitowoc. Their relationship developed and matured, even though one of them was human and the other one only partly so.

John and Nora grew even closer after she discovered — in the middle of a transplant operation — that the young man who was about to become Commando P-17 was none other than Cris Holman, the son she had been separated from since infancy. John guessed her secret, reluctantly agreed not to tell Cris, and helped Nora through her initial anguish by taking P-17 under his wing until the new commando demonstrated, by saving C-12's life, that he was quite capable of taking care of himself.

John didn't think he was going to make it back after being damaged, so he decided to reveal the truth about Nora to her son. In the months since then, the three of them had become like a family in many ways. The two men in her life were peers when it came to undertaking CC missions, but to Nora they were different indeed. Her love for Cris was the love of a mother; her love for John was the love of a woman — a love she could not feel in its entirety unless she held *him* in her arms. . . .

She walked across the room to where he could see her face, tried to convey her concern with her eyes, and waited for John to speak.

"I've been seriously considering doing some of these good drugs you people have been so kind as to add to my pharmaceutical inventory."

"Don't even joke about a thing like that, John."

"Hey, who's joking?" The cyborg's tone had a maniacal edge to it. "I mean, my mechanical brain dishes out the vitamins, nutrient supplements, hormones and stabilizers quite generously, and without my ever having to ask. But I know there's also a good supply of analgesics, antidepressants and tranquilizers stored somewhere inside this tidy little assemblage of nuts and bolts. Maybe my attitude would improve a little if I took a few thousand grams — or maybe the narrow-minded idiots who run this place could get me to do their bidding without asking any smartassed questions."

Nora let him ramble, listening patiently and compassionately.

"Tell you what — how 'bout adding some hallucinogens the next time you guys restock my medicine cabinet? Who knows, I might even imagine seeing enormous man-eating bugs chasing mechanical soldiers! Hell, I might . . . " John's voice choked with emotion, causing him to stop in mid-sentence.

"It's all right, John," Nora said softly. She had gone to the cyborg's side the minute he started to break down. She rested her hand on his forearm and squeezed gently, hoping the gesture and the pressure would do something for him even though he couldn't feel the tenderness from her heart that went along with it. John did feel the pressure and the warmth of her fingers, thanks to the sensory network that ran throughout his pseudoskin. Of course, it didn't feel the way it would have if his arm was made of living flesh. But the gesture and the feeling behind it didn't go unnoticed or unappreciated. John began to put his outburst behind him and regain his composure.

"You have every reason to feel the way you do right now," Nora said. "You've been fighting this war for a long time, with very little rest and very little to show for it. Do you want me to recommend that you be pulled from active duty for a while?"

The room was silent for a few minutes before John answered her question. "I don't think you'll have to. I was just put on suspended status by Major Fat-ass Williams for, of all things, insulting him to his piggy face." John looked at Nora and then, almost simultaneously, the two broke into fits of uproarious laughter.

Wiping the tears from her eyes, and working to stifle more giggles, Nora asked, "You mean you called"— a few errant chuckles interrupted the question, —"you called Major Williams a fat ass?" The mere thought of the obese major caused her to break down again.

"No, not in so many words. But I implied that if he were to apply that particular portion of his preponderous person to my super-resilient frame, it just might break!" That was all Nora needed to collapse in a heap of uninhibited mirth.

"Oh, John," she said when she was finally able to speak again. "I don't know why I ever worry about *your* mental state. You'll drive us all bonkers before you ever crack!"

John smiled. He felt better. Nora always made a difference in his outlook. If only their worlds hadn't been turned inside out, first by his becoming a CC and then by this xenoborg nightmare. Maybe, as normal humans in a normal world, they could have had a life together despite their age difference. Even as he thought this, John doubted it would ever have happened. With a seventeen-year gap standing between them, he probably wouldn't have made the attempt to get to know her and would have missed out on the most important relationship of his life.

"This is really frustrating, you know?" John remarked softly in the warm and gentle atmosphere that was the calm after the storm.

"What, John?" Nora asked. His tone implied that he wasn't referring to his present career problems.

"Oh, Nora. . . . I am so in love with you! I have been for a while now. And this thing . . . this thing my brain is trapped inside is keeping us at arm's length. But if it hadn't been for this," John said, indicating his mechanical body, "I probably would never have met you."

"I'm not sure we should be talking about love at this point," Nora said gently.

"I think we should," John said, his voice almost pleading. "I think we should be realistic about it. But I also think we should acknowledge it. I'm sure Major Williams is going to be persuaded to let me out of my room and back on the force as soon as General Garrison hears about what he did. And then I'm going to be going out there — by myself — on an assignment that could be the last for both John Edwards and C-12." Nora tried to quiet him, but John insisted on finishing what he had to say.

"I'm not sure C-12 cares about that, but John Edwards wants to live to see a better day. He wants to marry you some day!"

"Oh, John," Nora said sadly. "I love you, too. And I worry about you all the time. I want you to live to see better days. But assuming the best — assuming there is an end to all of this, and that all of us can pick up where we left off — there is no way you and I could live as husband and wife. "

"Why not?" John demanded.

"For starters, I have a son who's only a few years younger than you. That fact alone is enough to kill any hope of a normal male-female relationship between the two of us."

"So who says we have to be normal? Nora, if this whole, crazy, horrible nightmare has taught me anything, it's that every precious moment we have left after this should be spent the way we want — regardless of what anyone but the two of us thinks."

"But what about children?"

"Are you kidding? Do you think I'd bring children into this world after what I've seen in the last fourteen months? Hell, no! I'll leave procreation duty to any of my comrades who still think it's a good idea. All I want out of the rest of my life is to spend it with you and Cris."

Nora shook her head sadly. "You'd have a stepson almost as old as you."

"So, I won't require him to call me daddy.

C'mon, babe, will you at least think about it?"

Nora looked at John, and her heart almost broke. Of course she wanted to spend her life with him. But it wouldn't be fair to him. He'd end up having to care for her, an old woman, while he was still in his prime. But, oh, those first several years would be heaven. . . .

"Nora please. I need you to at least promise to consider my proposal. If I know you'll at least think about it, I'll have something to keep me going—"

"I'll think about it, John. But all I want right now is to know you'll come back here in one piece. You promise me that you won't let this . . . this runaway take any chunks out of you!"

"I think we have a deal, love." John barely got the words out of his mouth before his videocom began beeping.

C-12 walked over to the set and turned it on. The fleshy face of a humiliated Loren Williams nearly filled the screen. "Uh . . . Lieutenant C-12, you are wanted in briefing room three . . . immediately. Your confinement is hereby cancelled." Then the major, looking like he was about to burst, added a personal postscript. "But by God, you little shit, if you ever—"

John clicked off the set. "Guess I'm off to war again."

"Please be careful, John. And, no matter what we decide, I *do* love you. And I always will." Nora got on her toes, stretched as high as she could, and kissed the pseudoskin on C-12's cheek. John Edwards felt it physically, but, as always, there was something missing. . . .

"Save those lips for when I have my real mouth back, babe," John said happily, and then added softly, "and do me a favor? Leave a candle in the window, okay, love? I promise you, I will return."

5

April 21-22, 2036

Cris had a lot of trouble paying attention to the last few minutes of the briefing, because he couldn't wait to ask Tony dozens of questions that were running through his mind. Cris's preoccupation did not go unnoticed by Traynor. "Why don't we take a break so you two can catch up on each other's lives?" he suggested. "Then, P-17, maybe I can have your undivided attention?"

"Uh, sorry. But I just can't believe this. You have to at least give me a few minutes to adjust to the shock."

"I'll do better than that. I'll give you exactly two hours. Then I want the two of you back here, and I want your full attention."

When they were finally secluded in Cris's quarters, his questions came fast and furious. Tony, who couldn't resist the opportunity to have a little fun, obliged him with rapid-fire answers that only served to confuse Cris even more.

"How did you get into that body?"

"The same way you got into yours, pal."

"But you were turned down . . ."

"Yep. I *was*."

"And they told me you were being transferred to New Orleans. I even said good-bye to you."

"They weren't lying. It's a lovely city, or at least it used to be."

"Then how . . . ?"

"Let me get a couple of paragraphs in edgewise, okay? If you keep up this chaotic line of questioning, you'll use up our whole two hours and you won't learn a thing."

"Okay, but c'mon, what do you expect? I never expected to see you wearing one of these high-tech costumes!"

"Yeah, well, I can't say I expected to be dressed like this either. Now listen up, lieutenant — boy, I've always wanted to say that."

"All right. You have my full and undivided attention, *corporal*. . . ."

Tony Minelli and Cris Holman got to know each other in the days following the xenoborg invasion on January 13, 2035. At that time Cris was so griefstricken over the horribly brutal deaths of his father, stepmother, and fiancée that he was barely able to function, let alone manage to deal with a new friendship. But Tony was patient.

Cris had devoted most of his time and energy to caring for his small sister Sara, who had witnessed her parents' deaths when xenoborgs attacked their house. Sara never recovered from that shock and ended up losing her life while being transported to a safer victim relief center. Cris, who was not with her at the time, had blamed himself for her death and had vowed not to rest until every last one of the murderous invaders was wiped off the face of the earth.

Tony had provided Cris with a strong shoulder to lean on through all of this, although Cris resisted his friendship at first. The two went through Cyborg Commando candidate testing together a short time after their relationship finally got off the ground. But it seemed doomed when Cris was accepted for the program and Tony was turned down. However, they were able to stay in touch because Tony was given a job as a technical assistant at the Manitowoc base where Cris was stationed.

They had been separated — for good, or so they thought — last November. Tony and several other members of the Manitowoc staff were reassigned to the New Orleans base. The influx of CC candidates in the southern city was greater than the ability of existing personnel to process and train them. Manitowoc, being in a less densely populated area, had personnel it could spare. A lottery was held among all of the potential transferees, and Tony's number came up.

The last time Cris had heard anything about Tony was about a week after he had left, when Manitowoc got a brief message from New Orleans that all of the reassigned personnel had arrived safely. Because radio transmissions for personal purposes were absolutely forbidden, Cris and Tony had no way of contacting each other. Cris gave up on ever seeing his friend again and had tried to put him out of his mind. He hoped that for his own sake Tony would do the same thing.

"You know me," Tony said. "Always the optimist. I told my story of woe to anybody who would listen, figuring that maybe the rules were a little different down south. 'I really wanna be a CC,' I said, 'and I don't care if my body dies in cold storage. If you had a body like this, would *you* care?'

"Well, the right people finally listened to me. They said, 'Okay. If you don't care, then we don't care.' Actually, I think they *did* change the rules — they decided not to be as particular as they used to be about who could undergo the transplant, because the world needs all the Cyborg Commandos it can get right now."

"That's taking a big chance," Cris said. "What happens if they find out how to put brains back into bodies and you don't have a body to go back to?"

"I'll cross that chasm when I come to it. Right now it's not worth worrying about. Anyway, they told me just before I left New Orleans that my body was doing just fine."

"So why are you back here? How did you get here?"

"Questions, questions. . . . I'm here because I got *assigned* here. The system works in strange and mysterious ways, pal, in case you hadn't already noticed. They needed two CCs to ride shotgun for six medical types that were being shifted to work up here. I understand you've already met Doctor Higgins; well, he was one of 'em.

"I guess you wouldn't know, 'cause you haven't gotten around much, but it's not all that tough to get from one place to another any more. The xenoborgs don't usually mess with single vehicles; they've mostly dug in around big cities and CC base locations, and they aren't roaming the countryside like they did in the early days. So as long as you don't make too big a thing of it and stay off the major highways, you can take a truck just about anywhere you want."

"I may not have traveled very much," said Cris, "but I do know what's going on around me. Xenoborgs don't come out after us any more like they used to; they make us come to them."

"Two reasons for that," Tony chimed in authoritatively. "Most of the time, a single CC can fry two or three xenoborgs without even getting his hands dirty. And the xenoborgs know there are a whole lot of them and not very many of us. Time is on their side."

"Yeah, that's basically what the general said."

"Huh?"

"Oh . . . it's not important." Recalling his instructions, Cris tried to dismiss the subject casually. Tony seemed to have a good overall grasp of the situation, but Cris wasn't sure if Tony knew, or was supposed to know, all the details that General Garrison had revealed to him and John. "Tell me about this body of yours," he added, anxious to steer the conversation in a different direction.

"I can remember times in my former incarnation when I would have loved to hear a female ask me that question, but I guess you'll have to do." Tony sat on the floor. Cris heard the telltale clicks again, and a moment later the upper half of S-24's body was moving around the room, propelling itself by taking "steps" with its arms and hands.

"This thing on the bottom is what they call a universal socket," Tony said. "Since there's nothing below the hips that a CC actually needs to survive, they finally hit on the idea of making the torso interchangeable with different kinds of bases. Depending on what they need me to do, I can be hooked into a set of treads, a paddlewheel gizmo for moving through water, an air-jet unit for vertical jumps, or about a dozen other things. Plus, of course, the same old, more-or-less-normal legs that you've got for standard equipment."

"I'm jealous," said Cris, "even though it seems a little . . . unnatural."

"Well, just what *is* natural about a body where

the brain is in the chest instead of the head? If you can live with that — and you seem to be doing just fine — then you ought to be able to cope with the idea of detachable legs."

"Now you're starting to sound like Traynor."

"If you don't mind, pal, I choose to consider that a compliment."

Cris and Tony were interrupted by the alarm they had set to remind them to go back for the rest of their briefing. S-24 put himself back together, and then he and P-17 took off for their meeting with Traynor.

"Hey, buddy, do you know how many times in the last few months I've wished I'd see your anemic-looking body walk through the door?" Cris asked as they approached the briefing room. His tone did little to hide the emotion that was welling up inside of him.

"Sorry, pal. It'll be a while before that happens — if ever. Until then, will you settle for the new, improved macho Tony?"

Cris laughed. "You're still skinnier than me, you old S-model you."

"Yeah, well, what can I say? I guess some things never change."

6

April 24, 2036

The last reading on R-9 that had been received at the Manitowoc base had identified the cyborg's location as about fifteen miles north of the city. John set off in that direction alone the morning after his final briefing, conducted by three officers including Major Williams. The memory of his last conversation with the major the night before gave John a sadistic sense of satisfaction. The man had been forced to apologize to Lieutenant Edwards for having lost his temper, and it had been an ordeal for Williams from start to finish. John grinned involuntarily every time the picture of the major's chubby face, the most brilliant red John had ever seen in a skin color, flashed through his mind.

"I regret, Lieutenant Edwards, having lost my temper with you two days ago. That kind of behavior is beneath my rank, and I assure you it will never happen again." The words were delivered immediately following the briefing in the presence of General Garrison, who had ordered the apology.

Well, it wasn't actually an apology; after all, the man never said "I'm sorry" or anything close to that. The massive major is lucky that I was the person on the other end of that rope, John thought to himself as he trudged slowly along, using his scanner to attempt to trace the mechanical miscreant's location. Anyone else would have given the fat slob a hard time — but no, not good, old kind-hearted John T. Edwards. That thought made the cyborg laugh out loud.

In fact, John had readily accepted the "apology," much to Major Williams's relief. But when John turned to follow General Garrison out of the room after the final briefing, after making sure the general was no longer within earshot, he had casually tossed back, "Hey, pal, don't sweat it, really. From what I hear, they don't intend to demote you, or anything that severe. I think what they have in mind is cutting your calories, not your rank. That way if you ever screw up again, they won't have to remove any doors before they throw you out."

With that, John had made a hasty exit, not even daring to take the time to catch a glimpse of the fuming major. "But I could swear I smelled smoke still coming out of that room when I walked by it on my way out this morning," John said with a chuckle. Then he silently reprimanded himself: Come on,

Edwards, you have a job to do. This is not the time to get off on prior acts of brilliance.

John realized he was talking to himself a lot because he was having a hard time adjusting to his solitary status. He understood why this had to be a one-man mission, but still he found himself wishing that someone, preferably Cris, had been assigned to accompany him. John was lonely, but even more than that, he was worried about how Cris was doing without him. "The kid would forget his brain if it wasn't packed so tightly inside his chest," he mumbled.

He kept trying to stay lighthearted, but it wasn't working. "I wish to hell they had told me where he was going and what he was going to be doing! Shit!" John cursed softly as he stumbled over a tree stump and almost toppled over.

I just have to find this R-9 person and get him or her back to the base so that Cris and I can get back to our normal routine, he thought, trying to get his emotions back under control. "Normal? Hell, what is normal any more?" He pondered that question silently and bitterly. "Normal" these days, compared to what had been considered normal a little more than a year ago, were now worlds away in definition. It was a wonder the word was actually still in use.

"Okay," he told himself, "let's not sink into the depths of despair over the state of the world. One thing at a time." He tried to shake off his negative feelings and concentrate on the task at hand, especially now that he was getting fairly close to the last known location of the out-of-control Cyborg Commando.

Although he had been told about the problems he might have when he found R-9, he had no idea which of those he would be facing.

"This is a tricky situation because we don't know exactly what we're dealing with here," Williams's assistant, Captain Donald Britton, had told John during his briefing. "If the organic brain is dead and the autonomous body functions are being controlled by its internal computer, then we should have been able to lock onto it with a homing signal and bring it back in by now. However, it's possible that if the brain is dead, then whatever killed it also caused damage to the internal computer, and that's why we haven't been able to get it to respond to a signal or communicate with us.

"If the brain is simply unconscious, and if R-9 was able to put the machine on autopilot before he blacked out, then the internal computer would activate motors and sensors as needed to cause the body to avoid obstacles and attacks. This mode of operation is costly in power, and the electromagnetic radiation put out by the autopilot is easily detectable from fairly short range by the appropriate sensors. So there's a possibility that R-9 is running low on power and that it is being tracked by xenoborgs carrying sensors, which means you might find R-9 and at the same time encounter an enemy force. In this case, your main responsibility is to rescue and recover the unit or, failing that, to render it immobile so that it can't unwittingly lead the enemy to any sensitive location, such as this base.

"Another possibility, and a most unpleasant one, is that R-9 has somehow lost a great deal of power all at once and that the logic circuitry and information banks in its internal computer have been damaged as a result. In this case, what we have is a conscious, thinking Cyborg Commando that is capable of taking action and making decisions but is incapable of distinguishing between logical and illogical actions."

"In other words," John had interrupted, "it's a crazyborg."

"That's one way of putting it," the captain had continued. "But do not make light of this situation when you're in the field, lieutenant. We don't know what an irrational Cyborg Commando is capable of, so we must assume that it can do virtually whatever it wants, within the limitations of its body mechanisms, weaponry, and defense systems. Ordinarily, the internal computer would not allow it to train a weapon on you or take any other sort of offensive action against you. But in an irrational state, with both its organic brain and its electronic brain functioning improperly. . . ."

"I see," John said, sincerely serious. He fully

understood what the captain was getting at — R-9 might be able to open fire on him, but his own internal computer would probably not let him reciprocate. "This might be anything but a fair fight," he added, his sense of humor stepping aside to make room for his sense of survival.

"Which is why we think you're the best chance we have of succeeding on this mission," the captain said. "You have more combat experience than any other Cyborg Commando based at Manitowoc — possibly more than any other unit in the world."

"Why don't I get a partner, a backup?" John asked. He had hoped that subject would be addressed in the briefing, but since it had not been touched upon so far, he decided to bring it up.

"Two reasons," said General Garrison gruffly, rising from the chair he had occupied off to the side. "If it turns out to be just a tracking and recovery mission, a second unit would be redundant. One can do the job just as well as two. And if it turns out to be more dangerous than that, then we've kept our losses to a minimum."

"Right. So I get to be the guinea pig, huh?"

"Wrong," said the captain before the general could respond. "A guinea pig has no control over what happens to it." General Garrison sat back, apparently satisfied with that answer.

"What will happen to the person inside the machine when and if I am able to round him up and bring him in?" John had asked next, sensing the answer even before the question left the diaphragm in the back of his neck.

"We'll salvage what we can of the unit's equipment." Major Williams had shot out the answer to John's question with what John thought was an obvious air of detachment.

"This *unit*," John had said quietly and angrily, "contains what is left of a human being. Are you telling me that you people no longer place any value on a human life?"

"Now, look—" Williams had started to answer, but he was cut off in mid-sentence.

"The survival of the human race is our number-one priority, Lieutenant Edwards," General Garrison had said with quiet sincerity. "That's what the Cyborg Commando program is all about. That's what you and others like you have risked your lives for. But we have to be concerned about numbers here, and if one, lone, off-kilter cyborg is going to endanger a large number of humans, then it is in the best interests of the human race to see to it that it is stopped.

"And, if you'll recall the substance of our earlier meeting, it is crucially important for us to create and train as many Cyborg Commandos as we can. If this unit is allowed to run around wreaking havoc wherever it goes for as long as it remains operational, it will not only endanger lives but also deal a serious blow to our recruitment program. Having an uncontrollable unit traipsing around the countryside is, shall we say, not exactly beneficial to the image of the Cyborg Commando Force. Do you understand all that, lieutenant?"

"Yes sir," John had answered quietly.

"Lieutenant, I hope you also understand that if we are forced to choose between the man and the machine"— Britton paused briefly before continuing —"then I'm afraid we'd have to save the equipment. We have no choice at this point."

John replayed all of this in his mind as he trudged over the grassy terrain, through what had not too long ago been a cow pasture. In the distance small trees and bushes dotted the hillside. The sun was high in the sky, and John imagined another time — another bygone era, it seemed — when he would have been quietly thrilled to be taking a walk on a pleasant day such as this. He wondered if he'd ever have the opportunity to fully enjoy such a simple pleasure again.

John proceeded very slowly, scanning the area, using all four lenses in each eye and shifting the digital encoding and filtering system that allowed him to hear at human range, to wide-band hearing. The lenses and image processors in C-12's eyes covered a wide portion of the electromagnetic spectrum. By cycling rapidly between all his modes of "sight," he could pick up any telltale signals within a millisecond of the time he first encountered them.

John methodically and thoroughly checked out

every bush and building within five miles. He found various living beings, including a hungry dog, a frightened teenager, and a cyborg patrol team. "C'mon, pal, where are you hiding?" he muttered softly, after several such discoveries.

As if in answer to his question, he suddenly began to pick up a massive, low-frequency sonic vibration — a "noise" well below the range of normal human hearing that could not have occurred in nature. He tried to trace the waves back to their source and realized they were coming from the vicinity of a large barn that was barely visible on the horizon about two miles away off to his right.

"This better not be another false alarm," he muttered as he turned in that direction and began a double-speed trot toward the structure.

It wasn't.

7

April 23, 2036

"I think I've got a fix on it," said Cris. "About a thousand yards away, almost directly east."

Tony lifted his head up to the rim of a low concrete barrier and stared in the direction Cris had indicated, briefly activating his own infrared sensors as he did so. "Holy shit! That's either a massive living alien body or the world's biggest campfire!" Tony whistled in agreement.

They couldn't see the object with the part of their sensory network that operated in the normal visible spectrum. For one thing, it was about four hours after sunset and the sky was overcast. For another, the teleborg they were keying in on was almost completely obscured by concrete and metal buildings, at least from the vantage point that P-17 and S-24 had taken up. But the creature gave off heat, radiation in the infrared spectrum, that pervaded the air immediately around the thing and made its location readily apparent when the CCs trained their infrared sensors in the right direction.

Cris and Tony were on the northwestern fringe of what remained of the metropolitan area of Milwaukee, Wisconsin — one of several dozen urban environments around the world that had been first assaulted and then occupied by extensive, organized forces of xenoborgs and their supporting teleborg bases. Even under these dire circumstances, the surviving residents of Milwaukee and the other occupied cities might be considered fortunate; the populations of several dozen other urban areas, including most of the largest ones — New York, London, Tokyo, Chicago — had been practically obliterated in the first, overwhelming wave of the invasion.

According to Earth's military specialists, the occupations seemed to have two goals. There was the obvious strategic benefit of taking and holding many of the cities that had not been depopulated. Also, the show of force that the aliens were staging in such places had a devastating effect on the morale of those who were inside the perimeter as well as those who, desperately or unwittingly, tried to penetrate it.

As numerous as they were, the xenoborgs were still vastly outnumbered by the members of the human race who had not been killed in the early

days of the onslaught. But by stationing themselves in and around the remaining areas of highest population density, they made the most effective use of their hundreds of thousands of troops.
Slowly but inexorably, the noose was being drawn
tighter and tighter around the neck of humanity.

Xenoborg squads still went out on combat for-
ays, and they were liable to be found anywhere, in
rural and urban areas alike. But most of the invaders simply bided their time in and around the cities
of Earth. Instead of wreaking death and destruction
indiscriminately, now they were killing humans only
when they needed to eat or when they were ordered to forage and bring back nourishment for the
nearest teleborg. Otherwise, they simply waited for
the rest of the human race to die from starvation or
disease. In between excursions for food, the xenoborgs composing each occupation force re-
trenched and clustered around the nearest teleborg. These massive, immobile hulks, estimated to
number between two and three thousand worldwide, had probably not killed all told more than ten
thousand people themselves. But in their way, they
represented even more of a threat to humanity
than did the hordes of xenoborgs.

Each teleborg was equipped with anywhere
from one dozen to three dozen tentacles, depending on the size of its body, and also had from one
dozen to three dozen technological weapons —
lasers, grenade launchers, explosive missiles,

flamethrowers, radiation beamers. Even if all the xenoborgs on the planet suddenly shriveled up and died, it would take a massive expenditure of men and materials — including Cyborg Commandos — to disable or destroy every teleborg. As long as even a few of these unearthly strongholds remained, Earth would never be safe.

The prognosis that Cris had heard from General Higgins indicated that about four years from the start of the invasion, the enemy's double-edged strategy of brutality and attrition would all but exterminate the human race. Clearly, four years was not a long time in the invaders' frame of reference — and it was a pitifully short time for mankind to plummet all the way from a position of dominance on the planet to no position at all.

For the human race to have any hope, the invaders' stranglehold on Earth's major cities had to be broken, and one of the keys to accomplishing that was to confront and defeat the teleborgs. That task had seemed impossible at first, but finally scientists and strategists had hit on a plan that might work — and Tony and Cris were just about to see whether or not it would.

Having located their target, P-17 and S-24 made their way back down from the rooftop they had occupied. While keeping their eyes open for roving xenoborgs, they moved silently and methodically toward the teleborg, looking for a place where Tony could get beneath the surface.

"Psst!" Cris whispered. "To your left!"

Tony quickly ducked down behind the corner of an exterior wall, and Cris did the same a few feet away. They both remained crouched, not saying a word, for several minutes, while the shuffling sound of moving xenoborgs grew louder and louder. Finally three of the creatures came into view, moving in single file on an oblique angle in front of and away from where Cris and Tony were hiding.

Cris was relieved to see that the creatures weren't carrying weapons — or, if they were, the devices were in retracted positions beneath the monsters' outer skins. He wasn't worried for his safety; he knew that he and Tony could have chopped and fried all three of these things in a matter of minutes if they had wanted to. But they weren't supposed to attract any attention, and the xenoborgs' nonbelligerent attitude indicated that the monsters were not aware of their presence.

When Cris saw what the middle xenoborg was carrying, he had to fight with himself to keep from disobeying orders, stepping out from concealment, and blasting all three of the things to smithereens. Two of its tentacles, on the side closer to Cris, were wrapped tightly around the lower body of a man who was obviously dead. His head, arms, and battered torso were dangling beside the monster, bouncing against the ground as the xenoborg moved along. "Just like a piece of meat," Cris muttered under his breath. Then he silently chided himself — of course, that was *exactly* what the poor soul was to these creatures, and there was nothing he could do about that. He had to stop looking at things so emotionally, had to stop being personally outraged every time he witnessed someone being killed and devoured. He could almost hear John telling him to "Toughen up, kid!"

Devoured . . . that word raised a question in Cris's mind. Why hadn't these monsters simply consumed the man after killing him? Since they were heading in the general direction of the teleborg that Cris and Tony had spotted, there could be only one answer. Because the teleborg must have exhausted all of the food supply around it by now, xenoborgs were bringing food to the thing. "Maybe those creeps will take an edge off the creature's appetite before we even have a chance to get to it," Cris whispered to Tony. "If it rejects our offering—"

"We'd better get going," Tony whispered, having drawn the same conclusion that Cris did. Their mission would only succeed if they could get to the teleborg before it became satiated with other nourishment. One human being would not be enough to satisfy the appetite of such an enormous creature, but it might tend to make it feed less ravenously on the mass quantities of nutrients Cris and Tony hoped it would fill up on.

It was not easy to cover even a short distance quickly, because Cris and Tony had to keep from being seen or drawn into combat. If any xenoborgs did notice P-17 and S-24, the monsters would probably not initiate a fight; the creatures had long since learned, or been instructed, to give CCs a wide berth whenever possible. But they could, and certainly would, relay information to the teleborg about Cris and Tony's location, and the teleborg would not hesitate to fire on them if it knew where to aim. Even if they escaped being hit, they would then have to deal with a teleborg that had been put on alert, and that alone could be enough to spoil the plan.

So, as time-consuming as it was, Cris and Tony had to stay hidden while they inched their way along. They had to stay shoulder to shoulder most of the time, so that when they had to communicate, they could do so by whispering. They couldn't use their radios to stay in touch; they couldn't use their sonic projectors to help them "see" obstacles in the darkness; they couldn't use any device that gave off energy of any sort, because the xenoborgs or the teleborg itself might be able to pick up the signal and thereby trace their location. For this stage of the operation, all the technology and gadgetry of their cybernetic bodies was practically useless. They had to rely on sight, hearing, and touch to find their way around — just as a pair of normal human beings would do.

Locating an underground passageway was no problem; all they had to do was follow the east-west streets in the direction they were headed. They knew that beneath the streets would be storm sewers, water mains, conduits for power lines, and plenty of other tunnels heading eastward toward the teleborg. But they had no way of knowing which subterranean passages were unblocked and which ones would allow Tony to take the most direct route to a spot just beneath the teleborg. To give S-24 the best chance of getting down, doing his job, and getting back up again, they had to creep to within a hundred yards of where the teleborg sat — closer, if possible.

Traveling in a zigzag path to take advantage of the best cover and stopping three more times to avoid contact with xenoborgs shuffling through the streets, it took Cris and Tony more than an hour to travel the last several hundred yards to a spot where they could almost feel the teleborg breathing down their necks. A long, low, steel-and-concrete building was the only large object in a direct line of sight between them and the teleborg. If they tried to get any closer, they would defeat their purpose. They weren't here to trade punches with the teleborg — what they wanted to do was get in a good shot on its blind side before the creature knew what had hit it.

It wasn't necessary for Cris and Tony to exchange words; they both knew what they had to do. Tony pointed down to the manhole cover at his feet — he needed Cris to lift it, because he wasn't sure his own upper body was strong enough to pull it up as smoothly and silently as it had to be done.

Cris squatted down over the circular metal plate, gripped the small openings on opposite sides of the rim, and pulled the cover directly up. He winced as the metal rim scraped against the surrounding concrete — a brief noise, but one that sounded unbearably loud against the backdrop of heavy silence all around them. He resisted the urge to freeze and listen to find out whether the sound had attracted any attention, realizing that there was no turning back at this point. Even if they had been detected, the important thing now was to get Tony down into the passageway. If Cris had to hold off an attack and risk dying in the attempt, at least Tony would still have a chance of succeeding in his part of the mission.

Cris gingerly set down the manhole cover a couple of feet away from the hole. Tony lowered his body into a sitting position on the street. A second later he had detached his torso from his hips and legs. He moved to the rim of the hole, "walking" on the palms of his hands. Cris bent over his friend, lifted him by the head, and lowered him into the hole so that Tony could wrap his fingers around the ladder that led down. S-24 descended rapidly, hand over hand, into the dark hole. Cris peered down into the opening, and a couple of seconds later saw the soft glow of a light that illuminated S-24 and the part of the tunnel that he could see heading off to the east. Then the light went off again, and Tony climbed back up the ladder until his head was peeking out above street level.

"A little obstruction in the distance," he whispered, "but I'm pretty sure I can get around it."

"May as well give it a try," Cris breathed, reaching down to rest a hand lightly on S-24's shoulder. "I'll be right here. Hurry back."

"You can count on that," Tony said. "See you soon."

Without waiting for a reply, Tony lowered himself back into the hole. Cris saw the light come back on after Tony had reached the horizontal passage. Then S-24 started to head east, and silence and darkness descended on the area once more.

The Master was placid, complacent. As instructed, Its minions were now being methodical in their brutality — a slow determination exemplified by the indestructible outposts It had placed in areas of the planet that were still heavily populated. These stationary creatures were Its most formidable resource. They could not be dislodged, and their appetites could never be satisfied.

8

April 24, 2036

As John closed the distance between himself and the sound waves, the intensity of the "noise" grew rapidly. He could sense the disturbance of the air through which the sound waves were moving, and was able to pinpoint with increasingly greater accuracy where the sound was coming from. By altering his course slightly, he could put the barn between himself and the origin of the sound waves. Before he got close enough for his own body to be adversely affected by the vibrations, he would be able to use the structure as a shield — assuming that the barn remained in one piece for that length of time.

He found a small, dried-up streambed about a hundred yards away from the barn and dropped down into it, grateful for the relief it gave his auditory sensors to be out of the direct path of the vibrations. The gully ran roughly perpendicular to the path of the sound waves and curved in a gentle arc around the base of the ridge where the structure was located, so he started crawling to his left in an attempt to circle around and get a look at whatever stood between him and the barn.

Within a couple of minutes John had moved far enough to the side, out of the path of the sound waves, that he was able to get to his feet and move through the gully at a slow trot. The upper half of his body was visible above the level of the ground on his right side, but he figured that if he was seen and attacked from that side, he could throw himself down into the ditch before taking a hit.

Using what few facts he had in his possession, John tried to anticipate what he would encounter. The source of the sound waves could be a xenoborg, but it was generally believed that few of the monsters were equipped with such devices. Sound projectors were not very useful as weapons, except against objects that were nonliving and stationary, and xenoborgs tended to use attack forms that were more immediately lethal to humans, such as lasers and explosives. Still, the possibility could not be ruled out.

But it was much more likely that the source of the vibrations was another Cyborg Commando unit. Every CC had the ability to project sound waves. The tactic was useful as a form of sonar, at times when electromagnetic emanations might be detected; the waves would reflect off an object in the CC's path and perhaps even enable him to generally identify what sort of obstacle it was. Sound projection could also be used, as it was apparently being used here, to cause the target of the vibrations to shake itself to pieces.

Even as John recalled all of this in his mind, the barn began to creak and sway. It had held together for a remarkably long time, presumably because the wood was old and soft and thus had some "give" to it. But now the thing was on the verge of collapsing like a house of cards.

Just before he got to a place where he could see around to the back side of the barn, the wall nearest to him caved in. That caused the roof to come tumbling down, and before the top of the barn had settled completely to the ground its other three walls virtually disintegrated, sending chunks and splinters of wood spraying outward.

"Ah ha, ha, ha!"

John heard that booming, maniacal laugh an instant after he saw its source. Just a few yards away from where the back wall had been stood a Cyborg Commando, its arms upraised in triumph and its fists clenched. Pieces of the barn were scattered around its feet, and a couple of good-sized planks were wedged against the front of its body where they had come to rest after being catapulted outward by the weight of the collapsing roof.

John made a split-second decision, which turned out to be a wrong one. As the other cyborg's laughter faded, he raised a hand in greeting and shouted, "Hello! Good job, R-9!"

The sound startled the other CC. It turned its head toward John and saw the upper part of C-12's body about seventy yards away. It brought its arms down into laser-firing position and began to pivot its torso toward John at the same time. Fortunately, its movement was slightly hindered by a heavy plank that was leaning against its torso, and the extra half-second it took it to get its forearms pointed in the right direction gave John time to get out of the way.

C-12 dove for the safety of the ditch, hitting the ground just as two laser beams sizzled through the air in the place where he had been standing. "Damn!" he cursed, angry not at the CC who had fired at him but at himself for providing the provocation. If something scared the crap out of me, I might have done the same thing, he thought as he began to pull himself along the gully with his elbows, moving back the way he had come.

"Who is that?" the other CC boomed. Another pair of laser bursts scorched the earth a short distance behind where John's legs were located. "Give yourself up or I'll drill you!" A third shot cut through the air, this time several feet away from C-12. From that, John figured that the CC was firing blindly and wouldn't be able to tell exactly where

John was unless he did something to give himself away.

I can't show myself, John thought. If his override isn't working and he can shoot at me, then I'd be a goner. But the longer I stay hidden, the madder he's going to get. . . .

"Is that you, sir?" Suddenly the voice was not threatening, but laden with hope. John didn't know who "sir" was, but it was clear that R-9 was looking for an answer.

"Yes," John called out. "Hold your fire, R-9."

"Yes, sir!" came the crisp reply. John heard the noise of shifting debris and correctly assumed that R-9 was shuffling through the remains of the barn and making its way in John's direction. "Where are you, sir? Are you hurt?"

John got to his knees and raised his head above the edge of the ditch until he could see the landscape in front of him. R-9 was trotting down the slope, its arms at its sides. If I was an enemy, John thought, I could blow this guy to bits right now. He's either very trusting, or else he's . . . crazy.

"Over here," John shouted. Then, on impulse, he added, "My leg's a little messed up, but I'm okay." I'm less of a threat to him if I'm injured, he thought — and one thing I don't want to do is have him see me as a threat.

R-9 veered toward the sound of John's voice, and John pulled himself up over the edge of the gully, extending his right leg and being careful to keep it stiff, as though the knee joint was damaged. "Good to see you again, sir," R-9 said as it came up to where John lay, resting on one elbow.

This is the acid test, John thought. If he gets a real good look at me and decides, for some reason, that I'm not "sir," then one of us is not going to get out of this alive.

In the past, John Edwards had often bemoaned the fact that almost every Cyborg Commando looked like practically every other Cyborg Commando. He couldn't understand why each of the general-purpose models couldn't have at least some external characteristics that would enable people, and other CCs, to tell one apart from the others. Except for special models like the "S" series and the slight differences built in to distinguish males from females, they all looked alike. But now, for once in his life, he was grateful that faces and bodies were mass-produced instead of custom-crafted. R-9 was standing over him, peering down at him, and apparently was none the wiser.

"Let me help you up, sir," said R-9, bending down and reaching for John's left arm.

"Not just yet, R-9," said John, thinking fast. Before he committed himself to a course of action, he wanted to draw R-9 into some conversation, find out something about him, and gain his confidence. He still didn't have enough to go on. Right now, despite the pointless and irrational destructive act he had just performed, the guy seemed pretty normal. Just where *was* his head at? "If I don't use my leg for a while," he bluffed, "then it seems to get a little more powerful. I'd rather rest until I get some strength back."

"Of course. That makes perfect sense," R-9 agreed. "Can I make you more comfortable?"

"Not necessary, R-9. Why don't you fill me in on what you've been doing since . . . since we last saw each other?"

"I never thought I'd see you again. Stuck in a farmhouse that's going up in flames, surrounded by a dozen xenoborgs . . . how did you ever get away?"

"I hid in the basement until the place burned down and the monsters got bored and went away," John said, hoping to get away with yet another lie. How could he get this guy to stop asking questions and start answering some? Well . . . he was R-9's "superior officer," so maybe he could make it a direct order. "Now — what about you? I want a full report."

"Yessir," R-9 said. "I think I have something wrong inside, so I might not be able to remember everything, but I'll do my best. . . ."

John never found out how R-9 and "sir" managed to get themselves trapped inside a farmhouse and set upon by a large squad of xenoborgs, or why the leader had ordered his subordinate to evacuate before they got completely surrounded.

But when "sir" gave the order for him to "run like hell," R-9 had done just that. He took a couple of hits on the way out — probably what had damaged his internal computer circuitry. And then, apparently, something inside his organic brain had snapped. He was a relatively new recruit, alone in hostile territory, who had just been told to abandon his commander and leave him for dead. The stress and the guilt must have been too much for him to bear.

The more John heard, the less antagonism he felt for R-9. In fact, he could make a good case in his own mind for how the man's commander had brought on the whole unfortunate incident. By piling one bad decision on top of another one, he had left an inexperienced, insecure, and possibly unstable young man in a malfunctioning cybernetic body to fend for himself. Now, after almost three days alone in the field, the kid was starting to see xenoborgs behind every tree and under every rock — and that wasn't the only thing wrong with his perception of reality.

"I've been doing pretty well by myself," he said. "You know, those monsters can be hiding just about anywhere, just like at the farmhouse. I decided I wasn't going to get taken by surprise again, so every time I find one of their hiding places, I flatten it — like I did with that barn. Do you know how many of those things could hide in a place like that?"

"I can guess," John said sympathetically.

"Can't take any chances, sir," R-9 said proudly. "These things are getting smarter and more devious all the time. I saw one yesterday that looked just like a horse — it started to run toward me, and I blasted it. Why, I wouldn't be surprised if there were xenoborgs out here that look just like you and me. Can't be too careful."

Wow, John thought. This guy has really gone round the bend. I'm the one who'd better be careful. "Is that what you thought I was when you first saw me just now?"

"I wasn't sure, sir. And when I'm not sure, I shoot first and ask questions later," R-9 said confidently, as though he was sure that was the right thing to do.

"Why haven't you returned to the base by now?" John asked, trying to get some more useful information out of R-9.

"I've been trying," he said, "but I think my direction-finders are messed up. I get a fix on magnetic north, but a few minutes later something seems to shift around inside my head, and north isn't where it used to be any more."

John was relieved to hear that. The kid wouldn't be hard to handle, since he apparently did want to get back to headquarters. All I have to do is take him by the hand and limp for fifteen miles on my "bad" leg, he thought. Nothing to it. . . .

"I think I can walk now," John said. "And there's

nothing wrong with my sensors. Let's head for home, R-9."

"Gladly, sir!" the cyborg said exuberantly. John got up on one knee and was just about to pull himself to his feet when, to his astonishment, R-9 lunged out and pushed on John's chest with both hands.

"Get down, sir! Enemy units — coming over the ridge!"

9

April 24, 2036

Instinctively, John took R-9's warning at face value; if he resisted the push and pivoted to make his own assessment of what R-9 could see over John's shoulder — and if xenoborgs were approaching — then he would be vulnerable long enough to take a laser beam in the temple.

So he rolled in the direction of the thrust and threw himself back down into the ditch behind him. "I'll save us!" R-9 shouted. Before John could do anything about it, the other cyborg had shifted into ultraspeed mode and, his legs churning in a blur, was moving to take cover behind the remains of the destroyed barn. He threw out a couple of laser bursts as he ran, and the first one of them came within inches of hitting his intended target.

John got his body turned around to see what was approaching and froze in amazement for a second. Standing at the top of a small rise about two hundred yards away were a pair of Cyborg Commandos. One looked very much like C-12 and R-9 and most of the other CCs in the world; the other was thinner and shorter and had a set of treads below the waist instead of the usual hip-and-leg assembly. "Hold your fire, R-9! You're firing at our own units!" John said sharply, hoping that R-9 was in the mood to take orders.

"No, sir! These aren't any of our units, can't you see that? They're those bastard bugs in disguise," R-9 shot back excitedly and then added, "Stay down, sir. You're injured. I'll handle this one."

"No!" John shouted, to no avail. R-9 was not to be reasoned with.

Just after R-9's first laser attack scorched the air above the head of the smaller one, the two of them took off in opposite directions. The normal-looking one went into ultraspeed and moved down the slope at an angle, then suddenly disappeared from sight. John guessed that he had taken cover in another section of the gully in which he was lying. In the meantime, the one with the treads pivoted its torso one hundred eighty degrees and started moving in reverse back to the far side of the ridge. This one's movements were agonizingly deliberate compared to how fast a CC could move in ultraspeed mode, leading John to assume that this body — apparently one of the "S" series — didn't have high-speed capability.

By cocking his head to the left, John could see R-9 crouching down behind a portion of the wall of the barn that was still erect. The other CC aimed carefully and got off another shot just as the S-unit was disappearing behind the high ground.

"I think I hit it, sir!" R-9 shouted. "Did you see where the other one went?"

Thinking quickly, John lifted his right forearm up to the edge of the gully, aimed at a large rock about a hundred yards away out of R-9's line of sight, and fired. A second later, there was an ear-splitting crack as the rock fractured into hundreds of pieces.

"Got it!" John yelled. "It's all over, R-9!"

"Good job, sir! But we're not done yet. I'm going after the other one!"

"No!" John called out, but R-9 either didn't hear or wasn't listening. He darted out from behind the wreckage, went into ultraspeed again, and was in hot pursuit of the "enemy unit" before John could think of any way to prevent it.

"I never should have pulled that act about the bum leg," John muttered. "If he sees me up and running, my cover is blown — in more ways than one." He did the next best thing, pulling himself into a semi-crouch and starting to move along the ditch as fast as he could, trying to get to a place where he could at least catch sight of R-9 and the CC whom the "crazyborg" had begun to chase. The first thing John ran into, almost literally, was the Cyborg Commando he had supposedly killed a couple of minutes earlier.

This cyborg was slightly smaller in stature than C-12; the body was a bit more delicate-looking than his, but every bit as strong and well-equipped. He realized an instant after first seeing it that inside this body was the brain of a woman. She was sitting just on the other side of a sharp bend in the ditch, holding her left arm across her chest and feverishly trying to make some sort of adjustment inside the top of her left hand with her finger-tools. They noticed each other at about the same time just as John rounded the turn. She sprang to her feet, and John came to a halt just before he would have tumbled into her legs.

"What the *hell* is going on here?" she said. Her voice was metallic-sounding, making her words seem even more harsh than they were. "First your partner tries to cut us in half, and then you—"

"Get down!" John said in a stern whisper. "You're supposed to be dead!"

"What?" She couldn't believe what she had heard, but nevertheless she ducked back down. "Are my ears going bad again, or are you nuts?"

"Keep quiet and listen to me," he said, dropping to his knees and being careful to keep his head low. "The guy who shot at you is not my partner, but he *is* crazy. When he saw the two of you, he thought you were xenoborgs in disguise — and now he's taken off after the one that got away."

"Oh, no," she moaned. "You mean he's going to—"

"Unless your partner finds a place to hide or manages to figure out a way to defend himself, he's in big trouble."

"But how can he fire on another CC? The override—"

"The override is probably damaged, along with a lot of his other innards. And his real brain won't be any help, because his sense of reality is all out of whack. He's been seeing xenoborgs behind every blade of grass for the last few days."

"Then how did you—"

"I was sent out here to find him, render him harmless, and get him back to base. He thinks I'm his commanding officer, and we were getting along just fine until you—"

"All right. I get the idea. And you don't have to keep interrupting me!"

"We don't have a lot of time," John said, ignoring the outburst. "What do you want to do here?"

Before she could answer, a sharp cracking noise sounded in the distance, from the direction the other two cyborgs had taken. John suspected the worst — and his suspicions were confirmed a moment later when R-9 let out a loud whoop that reached his ears.

"Is that—"

"I'm afraid so," said John solemnly. "He found what he was looking for."

"That miserable . . ." she began, starting to get to her feet.

"No!" John grabbed her leg to keep her from rising. "If he sees you, then you and I are both in danger too! Your partner may be all right, but we'll never be able to get to him if we don't think of something — fast!"

She sat quiet and motionless for a minute; whether she was thinking or worrying about her partner, John couldn't tell. Suddenly she spoke. "Call him."

"Huh?"

"If you can hear him, he can hear you. Tell him to get back here on the double."

"Are *you* nuts?"

"Just do it," she said. "I feel another charge building up, and we don't have much time."

"Another charge?"

"Come *on*! Trust me!"

"R-9!" John shouted. "Come here fast! I'm hurt!"

"I got it, sir!" came the voice from the distance.

"Hurry!" John screamed.

"Yes, sir! I'm coming!" That reply was much louder than R-9's previous words, because R-9 was already much closer. The cyborg had shifted into ultraspeed mode again and was zooming toward the sound of John's voice as fast as he could. In about five seconds, John estimated, he would be over the rise, and a second or so after that he would be on top of them.

"Get way down," the woman said as she did the same, extending her left arm and hand so that only her index finger protruded above the edge of the ditch. John had no time to do anything but comply.

A second later, just as R-9 cleared the rise and roared down toward them, John smelled the telltale odor of ozone — as if a bolt of lightning had struck the ground a short distance away. Before he could think through what was happening, R-9 was no more than thirty feet away from where he and the woman were crouched. . . .

. . . And then he stopped, abruptly and silently.

That's it, thought John. He's spotted her, and now the game is over. Wondering if it was the last thing he would ever see, John raised his head out of the ditch to see what R-9 was doing.

He was doing nothing at all. The cyborg was frozen, his legs caught in mid-stride as though he had suffered some kind of instantaneous and total power loss. John put two and two together and figured out what had happened just as the woman leaped up and shouted, "It worked!"

"You shorted him out," John said in a tone half-way between a statement and a question. But she had already taken off in the direction of the place where her partner had been hiding. John followed and came up behind her just after she discovered the remains of her partner. From a short distance away, the unit looked undamaged, and it was even standing erect on its leg-treads. But as John drew closer, he saw two pencil-thin holes in the unit's torso and smelled the pungent odor of scorched flesh. That could only mean one thing: The cyborg had taken a laser hit that went right through its brain capsule. In organic as well as mechanical terms, the unit was quite dead.

"I'm sorry," John said sympathetically. "Would you like me to leave you alone?"

The cyborg didn't answer. She simply turned and walked back in the direction of the paralyzed unit. John followed, slowly inching his way alongside her. "I'm Lieutenant C-12, also known as John Edwards once upon a time—"

"My designation is O-33 — Sergeant O-33," the female CC shot back. Then, for a moment, a wave of emotion overcame her. "And I don't choose to remember any other time or place — or former name. Those days are gone forever, lieutenant."

John was quiet for a moment and then, as they neared the now harmless R-9, he asked, "How *did* you do that?"

"A massive overdose of electrons," she said. "A static charge of somewhere around fifty thousand volts, with nowhere to go except into his body."

"But how—" John asked, aware that a weapon of that magnitude was not standard CC equipment.

"I've been having trouble with static buildup in my left arm for the last few hours. In fact, I was in the process of trying to fix it when you found me. Every time I start to feel the tingling, I have to stop and find some conductive material I can use to bleed off the charge. This time, your R-9 just happened to be the nearest grounded object in the line of fire."

"But your override wouldn't—"

"Wouldn't let me fire at another CC," she again interrupted him before he had formed the full question. "But I didn't do that — I aimed the charge at where he was *going* instead of where he *was*. The override kicked in right after he ran into it, but by then the charge was depleted and the damage was done."

"Is he dead?"

"I'm not sure, but I don't think so. The brain is insulated and probably okay — maybe even still conscious — but all of the systems that the brain controls are burned out. And I wouldn't be surprised if the internal computer is fried. That was quite a jolt he took, and of course he had no chance to prepare for it."

"How long will he stay this way?"

"Well, even though I'm pretty good at field repair, I couldn't do a thing for him — even if I wanted to," she added grimly. "They might be able to salvage a few parts, but the only major portion of R-9 that's still viable is his brain. And based on the events of the last few minutes, even that may not be salvageable."

"Well," said John, "I guess this mission is over. And I have you to thank for that, sergeant." He made sure to emphasize her title, and then added gratefully, "I owe you my life, O-33."

"He didn't deserve to die," she said absentmindedly, looking back in the direction of the fallen CC. But before John had a chance to offer a sympathetic comment, she added — somewhat coldly, he thought — "Let's pick up the pieces and get the hell out of here, okay?"

10

April 23-24, 2036

From a military standpoint, what Cris had to do in the next several minutes — no longer than half an hour, he hoped — would be the easiest part of the mission. But from a psychological standpoint, it would be anything but simple.

While Tony made his way through the tunnel, risking his life every foot of the way, all Cris had to do was find a secluded spot within sight of the manhole and wait for his friend and comrade to reappear — wait, while the time passed with agonizing slowness and he had no way of being sure from one minute to the next that Tony was still okay. Considering the number of tentacles each of these creatures possessed, and considering the fact that many of these appendages reached down into the earth, there was a good possibility that S-

24 would get tangled up in one of them. If that happened, it was a certainty that the teleborg would crush or otherwise dismantle the cyborg and consume its organic parts.

Based on the distance Tony had to travel to get beneath the teleborg and then back out again, Cris would allow no more than an hour for S-24's head to pop back up out of the opening. If Tony had not returned by then, Cris's orders called for him to get out of the area and give S-24 up for dead. Orders or no orders, he wasn't sure he'd be able to do that if the time came, but for now he tried not to think about it.

Cris picked up S-24's lower body, cradled the legs across his forearms, and quickly headed for an office building along the south side of the street. The large glass door was shattered, so to enter silently all he had to do was duck his head and ease his way through the opening. Once inside, he chose a broken-out window on the northeast corner of the ground floor from where he had an unobstructed view of the street and the place where Tony had descended.

He sat on the floor facing the window, bent his knees, and pulled his upper body as close to the window as he could. Satisfied with what he could see from that position, he lifted S-24's leg-and-hip assembly up to his shoulders, as though he was about to give the strange-looking mechanism a piggy-back ride. He pointed the legs directly out in front of himself, locked the knee joints so the legs would remain straight, and rested the heels of the feet on the window sill. In this pose he looked very much like a man with an old-style bazooka launcher on each shoulder — and that was an appropriate comparison.

When they were detached from his upper body, each of S-24's legs could be used as a laser blaster. By opening a small cover behind each knee and touching his thumbs to the buttons he found inside, Cris activated the weapons. An almost imperceptible surge of current that he felt through the buttons themselves told Cris that the lasers were armed and ready to fire. If he pushed a little harder on the buttons, sizzling beams of coherent light would shoot out of the minuscule apertures on the bottom of each foot. He didn't have the advantage of computer-assisted aiming the way he did when he used his own built-in lasers, but he was still sure he could hit anything he saw.

S-24's "leg lasers" would be Cris's primary weapons for the time being, in case he needed to fight off anything that threatened him or tried to prevent Tony from getting out of the hole. The advantage to this was that he wouldn't need to deplete any of the power he needed to operate his internal weapons systems — which was important because he and Tony might need all the firepower he could bring to bear if they were later forced to battle their way out of this hostile territory and back to safety. Even if Cris used up all the power in the leg lasers, Tony would still be able to reattach the unit to his torso and move, because the batteries that provided motive power and those that operated the weapons were on different circuits.

After getting himself properly situated, Cris dropped his hands to his sides. He decided not to keep his thumbs poised on the buttons; if he was startled by something he might set off the lasers prematurely, betray his location, and put Tony in even more jeopardy than his friend already was.

Cris settled down and tried to force his mind to relax while still keeping his attention fixed on the street before him. A couple of minutes later, he had achieved a compromise between total, nerve-wracking tenseness and absolute lethargy. Suddenly, he was jolted into full alert by the telltale shuffling sound of an approaching xenoborg.

The noise, coming from the west, grew louder as the creature approached. Cris knew he had done nothing to give himself away, so he assumed that either the xenoborg was simply on a random patrol or it was purposefully heading toward the teleborg. He sat tight, still not bringing his thumbs up to the firing buttons, and watched as the monster came into view from his left, lurching its way down the middle of the street less than forty feet from where Cris was hidden.

If it turned in his direction, he would have to blast it, leap from hiding, and then take his chances; he couldn't afford to be caught inside the building and surrounded if there were other xenoborgs in the area. He tensed internally but didn't move, following the creature with his eyes.

It kept moving in a straight line perpendicular to Cris's line of sight and line of fire until the front of its body was hidden from Cris's view by its rear flank. Relief washed over him because, apparently, the thing had not noticed him. Then fear stabbed him like a hot knife as he realized what the xenoborg *had* noticed.

Cris had purposely left the cover off the manhole, realizing that Tony wouldn't be able to lift it easily by himself when he wanted to exit. Now he regretted that decision. The heavy metal disc was lying on the street, and either it or the circular hole nearby had attracted the monster's attention. Cris pressed the palms of his hands against the floor, lifted his body slightly, and pivoted himself and the leg lasers a bit to the right, putting the xenoborg once again directly in his line of fire.

By that time the creature had reached the hole and the cover. It paused, circled the area so that the front of its body was in Cris's view, and extended its tentacles toward the cover. With movements that seemed a combination of curiosity and apprehension, the thing ran the tips of its tentacles over and around the cover. It found one of the openings along the edge, thrust a tentacle into it, and lifted one side of the cover a few inches off the ground. Then the tentacle let loose — whether accidentally or purposely, Cris couldn't tell — and the cover hit the street again with a terrible clang that actually made Cris jump. His metallic hindquarters came off the floor and hit again with a thud, at the same time that his feet reflexively kicked out against the wall he was facing. Fortunately, the noise he made was masked by the softer clattering of the cover as it rotated against the concrete for a few seconds before coming to rest again.

Its examination of the cover seemingly complete, the xenoborg turned now to the hole, feeling around the edge in much the same way that it had done with the cover. Then the thing lowered a couple of its six-foot-long tentacles into the opening, as though trying to ascertain how deep it was.

And then, while Cris watched in dread and horror, the xenoborg started to pull its body down into the hole!

* * *

The bottom of the hole was damp, and in a few places there were small amounts of rancid standing water. The air was putrid and would have made a human being gag. None of that mattered to Cyborg Commando S-24, whose body was moistureproof and — when he wanted it to be, such as now — odorproof as well. But S-24's brain was human, and Tony Minelli had to suppress a feeling of mental nausea as he made his way along and through the three-foot-diameter passageway.

"This is no place for a person to be," Tony said softly to himself. "Which, on second thought, was exactly why they got good old metallic yours truly to do the job."

To the old Tony, chattering and joking was as essential to his nature as needing to eat and drink. Now that his brain was encased in a capsule inside an electromechanical body and drew all its sustenance from nutrients that were stored internally, Tony no longer required or even desired food and water. But he still needed to talk — and if talking to himself was the best he could manage, then that's what he would do.

Moving forward was tedious but not difficult. He assumed a face-down position with his arms extended over his head, then pressed down or against the sides of the tunnel with his elbows and pulled his torso forward until his forearms were tight against his chest or his sides. When he kept his chin up, as he did almost all of the time, a small, directional-beam lamp in his lower throat gave him enough light to see clearly for twenty feet, and he could make out objects of significant size from as far as fifty feet away.

He had weapons if he needed them — the same internal knuckle-lasers that P-17's body was equipped with, except that he could only fire a single beam instead of a double one. He also had microwave projectors in the palm of each hand, a feature that had become virtually standard equipment for all CCs once everyone discovered how effective they were against xenoborg flesh. And he had the full range of defense mechanisms and sensory receptors, so that he could take care of himself quite well if he had to.

But, for all that, S-24 was not expressly designed as a combat machine. Tony's claim to fame, and that of others like him, was their usefulness as guerrilla fighters, their ability to get into places where a standard-sized, standard-model CC couldn't go. With pneumatic drills and other digging tools clamped onto their upper extremities, they had been used to rescue people trapped inside demolished buildings and caved-in tunnels — dangerous places where an explosion, a laser blast, or the brute-force excavating of a standard CC might cause an even worse collapse of rubble and debris.

They got their share of actual combat duty, too. Tony still smiled to himself every time he recalled one of his first missions in New Orleans. While his partner took custody of his lower body, just as Cris had recently done, S-24 sprawled the rest of himself out on a plot of grassland and played dead. To xenoborgs that had never seen such a thing before, he looked like a CC who had been disabled, killed, and abandoned. So, instead of shying away from him, they came close to have a look, perhaps with the intent of taking the remains away to study them. But before they could wrap a single slimy tentacle around one of his spindly arms, his partner would start blasting away with both of his own lasers plus Tony's leg units.

The strategy worked like a charm the first time, and on several other occasions after that. Every one of the monsters died without ever realizing how they had been fooled, because Tony had never needed to use his own weapons. Then, one time, he and his partner found themselves biting off more than they could digest, and Tony had to join the fight to keep his partner from being caught in a crossfire between two laser-wielding xenoborgs. The ruse didn't work quite as well or as often after that, but in the meantime several CC pairs using the tactic had managed to kill off a few hundred monsters.

"I'll have to tell the bigwigs back in Manitowoc about that little trick when I get back," he muttered. "If it works as well everywhere else as it did in New Orleans, maybe . . ."

Tony stopped as he got his first good look at the "little obstruction" he had told Cris about. Twenty-five feet ahead of him in the passageway was a shape that was unmistakably human and definitely not moving.

He crept closer, knowing it would be pointless to call out a greeting. If anyone was alive and conscious down here, he or she would certainly not be sitting against the side of the tunnel enjoying the scenery. With a half-dozen more push-and-pull movements, he brought himself up to where he could, with his next extension, reach out and touch the body.

But he wasn't about to touch it if he didn't have to. The body was that of a small man, probably in his sixties — or older judging by the sparseness of the hair on his head. His knees were together and bent, both legs flopped languidly to the side away from Tony. His back rested against the curve of the tunnel wall, which apparently supported it well enough that he hadn't fallen over since he had died. His head hung to one side, pointing in the same direction as his knees, and his arms hung straight down at his sides. He wore a heavy cloth overcoat, too-large trousers, and shoes with no socks. Tony might have been able to estimate his age more closely — as if it mattered — by looking at the man's face.

The trouble was, he didn't have much of a face left.

The body was partially decomposed, and all of the exposed skin surfaces looked as if they had been gnawed or chewed by rodents and insects. Tony had always enjoyed horror movies in the old days, and had never had any trouble stomaching the most grisly visages that make-up artists could create. But this was different. This was real.

He tried to control his revulsion by keeping his

mind on the task at hand, and by talking to himself some more.

"Okay," he said. "I gotta get past him, and I don't want to just crawl right over him. But I can't go around, and I can't walk on the ceiling. So what *can* I do?"

He hit on a good idea after a few seconds of thought. He would have to touch the body, but he could keep it to a minimum. He inched as close as he could without actually coming into contact with the corpse, braced his left elbow against the curved wall of the tunnel for leverage, reached out and up with his right hand, and grabbed the left shoulder of the man's coat.

He pulled, ever so gently, and the man's upper torso began to slide across the rough-textured concrete toward him. Before it could fall far enough to touch him, Tony stopped the motion of his right arm, holding the body in place, and pulled his left elbow back a few inches, thus moving his own torso safely away from what was left of the man's head. With one more gentle tug, the speed of the man's fall overcame the friction of the wall, and he flopped down onto the floor of the tunnel, flat on his back, his eyeless face pointed toward the ceiling. The feet had also slid down to the floor in reaction to the movement of the upper body, but the knees were still bent and sticking up into Tony's crawl space.

"So far, so good," Tony told himself. Even

though he figured the fear was an irrational one, he was nonetheless greatly relieved when the man's head stayed attached to his body instead of coming loose and rolling across the tunnel floor. "Now," he said, trying to calm himself with a bit of bad humor, "I just hope his arms stay inside his sleeves."

Tony backed himself a short distance away from the man's head, then reached out and grabbed both shoulders of the coat. Using his elbows and the weight of his torso for leverage, he pulled the man's body toward him. With every few inches the body traveled, the man's knees unbent slightly and his legs became a bit straighter. Finally, the body was stretched out flat and more or less straight, roughly parallel to the sides of the tunnel.

Now it would be possible for Tony to get past the corpse by straddling it with his outstretched elbows, holding his torso up off the floor (and off the body), and "walking" with his elbows tightly pressed against the lower sides of the passage. He shuddered inside as his throat-light played over the length of the body while he made the gruesome five-and-a-half-foot journey.

"Looks like he was hiding down here for some reason," Tony said to himself, again using his voice to try to distract his mind. Then, realizing the man apparently had no food or personal effects with him, he advanced another theory. "Or . . . he got down and then couldn't get back up." He said that just as he got to the man's feet, and his light shone directly down on the gap between the trousers and the shoes — a gap filled only by the bones of the man's ankles.

"Damn," said Tony as he pulled his torso over the feet and brought himself back down to the floor of the tunnel. "I wish I hadn't thought of that."

By the time he resumed his normal mode of travel and had pulled himself another hundred feet or so toward the teleborg, Tony had been in the passageway for almost fifteen minutes. Fifty yards behind and about fifteen feet above him, an inquisitive xenoborg was trying to shove its bulky body into the manhole.

*　*　*

When he took a second to think about it, Cris realized there was no way the thing could get into the hole, at least not in its present condition. Even though the thing was small for its kind, it was still at least six feet in diameter along most of the length of its bulbous body — far too large to fit anything but its tapered front end inside the two-foot-diameter vertical hole.

But because it was small, it was also stupid; Cris and other CCs had learned a long time ago that the intelligence of a xenoborg was directly related to its size. Maybe it thought it could squeeze itself into the hole, and wouldn't give up until it got stuck. Then how would Tony get out?

Or maybe it had enough smarts to realize that if it changed shape, it could get into the passageway. Because of what he knew about shape-changing, he found himself almost hoping the creature would try to do just that — but what he really wanted was for the thing to lose interest and get the hell out of there.

Cris's experience with shape-changing xenoborgs dated back to the first day of the invasion — when he had still been Cris Holman, a defenseless but resourceful young male human being. After seeing his father and his stepmother grabbed and murdered by the monsters, he had escaped them by running into a dense cluster of trees where they could not follow. At least, he had *thought* they couldn't get in — until he saw them stop before his eyes and start to expel moisture. They were making themselves smaller, thinner, so they could get through the narrow spaces between the trees.

Fortunately, the process took a while, so on that occasion he had had plenty of time to outflank them and get away. And he had learned since then that when xenoborgs were shape-changing — whether expelling water to get smaller or taking it on to get larger — they were all but oblivious to their surroundings and very vulnerable to any sort of substantial attack. In fact, as he had found out after becoming a Cyborg Commando, Cris probably could have walked out of the trees that night and strolled right past the obscene, almost inert lumps. He might even have been able to kick them in their snouts and get away with it, although he wouldn't have done them any harm with such an ineffectual blow.

But now, with the essence of Cris Holman contained in a body that could kill a xenoborg in any of a half-dozen ways, he relished the opportunity to catch one of the monsters in the act. They were easy enough to kill when fully active, even when fully armed. Still, he would enjoy walking right up to one in the process of changing, kicking it in the snout, and frying it down to nothing while it simply sat there, helpless and almost senseless. . . .

The prospect was enticing, but Cris quickly came back to reality. He couldn't even kill a defenseless xenoborg without endangering the mission, not to mention Tony's safety. But now he had a second thought: Yes, it might actually be good for the xenoborg to start shape-changing — as long as the timing worked out right.

If the creature was occupied when Tony came back out of the hole, Cris could help him up, get him put back together, and the two of them could escape the area without incident . . . maybe. Cris wasn't worried about having to contend with a single xenoborg, but he was concerned about what might happen if the monster had a way of communicating with other xenoborgs — or, worse yet, with the teleborg. If the thing managed to get off some kind of distress signal before it got blasted, then he and Tony might be in big trouble.

If . . . if . . . if. Cris's objective side took over again, and he decided to just sit tight and see what developed. He hated not being in control, not knowing what would happen. But, like it or not, that was precisely his situation at the moment. All he could do was watch. . . .

. . . And as he watched, the xenoborg drew its snout back up out of the manhole! The thing had wegded itself into the opening so firmly that it had to actually twist its body as it pulled up. If there hadn't been so much at stake, the scene would have seemed comical to Cris. But all he cared about right now was seeing the thing get out of the hole and then lose interest in its discovery.

It did get out, with a slight popping sound that seemed louder than it was because of the pervasive silence. But then, instead of shuffling on its way, the thing settled down on top of the manhole cover. Within seconds, the dim moonlight revealed to Cris that the surface of the xenoborg's body was beginning to glisten with wetness.

That cinched it — the thing was going dormant and starting to change shape. Its outer skin was softening, and every cell of its body was devoting itself to the expulsion of all unnecessary moisture, until it had lengthened, narrowed, and reduced its bulk enough to get through the hole.

The water was coming out of the creature more rapidly all the time; already it was beginning to run off its body and form tiny puddles and streams on the street. Cris knew the changeover would take a while, because the thing had a lot of water to get rid of. But would it take long enough for Tony to get beneath the teleborg, deposit his "gift," and get back out again? Cris kept the leg lasers targeted on the xenoborg but fixed his eyes and ears on the hole, waiting and hoping for some sight or sound of Tony's return.

* * *

Once he got past the dead man, Tony made good progress. The tunnel was clear of any other sizable objects, and he happily discovered after traveling another few hundred feet that the passageway was gradually widening. Instead of having to pull himself along, now he could move by walking on his hands with his torso more or less erect. He couldn't go as fast as he wanted, or he would risk outrunning the range of his light, but he could travel at least twice as fast as he had before.

"Okay," he said. "Now we're getting somewhere. A couple more minutes at this pace, and I'll—"

He stopped short as his light caught a dark shape protruding down from the tunnel ceiling a few yards ahead. On a hunch, he activated his infrared sensors for a second. The object was thick, tapered, moving gently, definitely giving off heat . . . alive!

This was the first evidence of what he had been told to expect — one of the network of root-tentacles that the teleborg had put down beneath its body. The extremities served partly to anchor the creature and partly as a way for it to leech food from the earth.

What Tony had to do was get past the outermost roots until he found an area where the tentacles were fairly densely packed. Then, from a storage compartment inside his torso, he would take out the containers of super-concentrated organic nutrients he carried and spread them around where the tentacles could get at the stuff and start sucking it up. It was important to introduce the food to as many different root-tentacles as possible, so that it would spread through the teleborg's entire cell structure quickly. If the plan worked, the teleborg's biosystem would for a short time be so engrossed in assimilating and digesting the food that it would be unable to defend itself adequately — and during that time, it could be blasted from above while the thing savored its last meal.

A lot of things could go wrong with the plan, of course. Maybe the teleborg would not have bothered to send root-tentacles down into the tunnels and conduits that ran underneath the city. Maybe there would be no dense concentration of tentacles, so that only two or three roots would absorb the stuff and the teleborg's entire body would not be "paralyzed." Maybe the thing wouldn't like the feast that the scientists back at headquarters had prepared for it, and would try to munch on S-24 instead.

Tony knew about all of these potential problems, but, as he had said to Cris during their briefing, "A plan that might have holes in it is better than no plan at all." That remark came back to him now, as he crept toward the root-tentacle outlined in the glow of his throat-light. He was actually encouraged by its presence, since it meant that one of the possible holes in the plan didn't exist after all. The teleborg had indeed sent some roots into the tunnel system — no doubt in search of the water that had collected inside the passageways.

The root-tentacle seemed oblivious to light, but Tony was afraid it might be able to sense the vibrations of sound, so he kept quiet and moved with absolute silence up to where he could get a very good look at it. In size and shape, the end of the extremity that Tony could see very closely resembled an elephant's trunk. It was wriggling slowly, but the movement was stiff instead of fluid, because most of its outer surface was covered with a tough, fibrous material. The tip was light-colored, blunt, about three inches across, and had a texture that looked like wet, coarse cloth.

The tentacle was bobbing around randomly, poking and sliding the tip against the floor and sides of the tunnel. Occasionally it would hit on a small patch of water and pause briefly, and when it moved on it left only a stain of dampness behind. The thing was protruding through an elongated fissure in the ceiling, and directly beneath that opening was a smattering of earth and a few small chunks of concrete. Apparently the tentacle had found a crack in the tunnel, and the upper part of the root had enough strength to force the smaller end through the opening, rupturing it even more in the process.

Tony stayed out of range of its sweeping movements and watched it for a minute or so, wondering how he was going to get past the slowly flailing appendage without touching it — and wondering what would happen if he did come into contact with it. Then, abruptly, the thing stopped moving and simply dangled straight down from the crack in the ceiling. A couple of seconds later the tentacle drew straight up until the tip was a few inches above the floor of the tunnel. Then the extremity seemed to stiffen along its entire length, and the next thing Tony knew it was retracting back into the ground above the tunnel. He waited briefly until he was sure it wasn't lurking, waiting to pounce on him. Then he took a couple of giant steps with his forearms and got across the gap. After a brief glance backward and up at the crevice to see if his movement had somehow been detected, he moved on.

Over the next couple of hundred feet, Tony encountered only four more root-tentacles, but he also saw plenty of cracks and holes in the concrete that indicated other tentacles frequently penetrated the tunnel in this area. The extremities he did come across were fairly easy to circumvent, since they protruded from the sides and floor of the passageway instead of from the ceiling. Once, a squishy tip lurched out and actually brushed against him as he tried to edge his way past it, but the thing seemed not to notice him — S-24's body was not organic, and what the teleborg couldn't eat, it didn't care about.

After that incident, when Tony realized he was not in any immediate danger of being grabbed and devoured, his confidence increased with every step. And suddenly his spirits rose even higher when he finally came upon what he had been looking for.

Ahead of him the tunnel opened into a large chamber about forty feet in diameter, apparently a collection point into which several of the concrete passages spilled their contents. The ceiling of the chamber was practically shattered, the rubble from its destruction strewn all over the concave floor — and the center of the chamber was full of tentacles!

Tony felt like a tiny sea creature looking at the underside of a giant jellyfish. Most of the tentacles — there were at least a hundred of them all told, he guessed — were waving aimlessly with their tips a foot or two above the debris on the floor.

One or two in each small sector of the area were probing into the pile of rubble, looking for the places where water had collected.

As Tony watched, he figured out how the creature operated. When one of the searching tentacles found something to ingest, another five or ten of the extremities on "standby" right around that one promptly extended themselves and started to busily investigate the immediate area. From the frantic way the searchers were jerking around and the way the others rushed to a spot when something digestible was discovered, Tony figured he had caught the teleborg in the middle of a feeding frenzy — and that suited him just fine.

He started to make his way around the perimeter of the chamber, where the tentacles had not yet begun to search in earnest. He stopped periodically to open the compartment in his torso and take out one of the large capsules of nutrients. The capsules could be broken open by force, but they were also water-soluble, so all he had to do was find a small pocket of water the tentacles had not yet discovered and drop a capsule into it.

By the time he got back to his starting point and dropped the eighth and last capsule near the mouth of his escape tunnel, the searchers had already discovered water in the areas where he had made his first two drops. Water, and something more — something good!

Tony allowed himself a couple of minutes to savor the scene that was unfolding before him. Somehow, word was spreading that there was good stuff to be found around the edges of the chamber. One by one in rapid succession, the searchers stopped fishing around near the center, where the greatest concentrations of water would normally be found, and moved toward the walls. When one of them hit on a place where a nutrient capsule had dissolved, every other tentacle that could possibly reach the area shot out in that direction. Tony turned to leave just as the last of the food was discovered, only a few feet away from where he was positioned. But he could have been a mile away for all the teleborg cared — it was interested only in gorging itself.

"Suck it up, you slimy bastard," Tony muttered when he had gone far enough back along the tunnel so that the tentacles couldn't detect the sound waves. "It'll be the last thing you ever enjoy."

The trip back was a breeze. All the tentacles he had encountered on the way in had been withdrawn from the tunnel. Tony supposed that either they had found all the water they could find, or that they had been pulled back and redirected toward where the really good stuff was. Either way, he was glad he didn't have to contend with them, because he knew he was running short on time. If he didn't get out soon, Cris might not be waiting for him when he did emerge.

He was in such a hurry, in fact, that he didn't

bother to avoid the dead body on his way out. Instead, he shut off his light for a few seconds and ran directly over the man, his arms making long strides to get over the corpse in as few steps as possible. He tried not to think about what he was touching, and it helped not to be able to see it beneath him.

He flicked his light back on, kept up his rapid pace, and in another few seconds came to a halt beside the ladder that led up into the manhole he had earlier descended. He turned the light back off, so that the glow wouldn't be seen by anything prowling the street above him. Then he began to pull himself up the rungs slowly, and as he did so he noticed that they were wet — dripping, in fact.

He adjusted his audio sensors to extremely high sensitivity and ascended the last three rungs very deliberately, but all he could hear was the sharp splat of water droplets impacting on the ladder. Then he eased his head above the rim of the hole very gingerly — and stared directly at the flank of a xenoborg not more than three feet away.

11

Nora entered the lab and turned on the lights. Her meeting with Dr. Higgins wasn't scheduled to take place for a while yet, but she had just said goodbye to Cris and she wanted to get to work immediately, hoping her concentration would not be ruined by her concern for her son's safety.

"Don't worry, Nora," Tony had assured the anxious woman shortly before their departure. "I'll make sure he's home before curfew."

At least he's with someone who cares about him, Nora thought as she sat down and opened one of the ledgers she had brought with her. Even though it was unreasonable and unrealistic to expect that Cris and John would always be paired whenever a dangerous mission came up, she still wished they had not been split up. And if both of these missions had not become necessary at the same time, she thought, then at least one or the other of them would still be on routine patrol duty.

"Fate works in strange and cruel ways," she murmured to herself, trying to be philosophical. "And there's nothing I can do about it except try to look at the good side." Both of the men she loved were among the best in the world at what they did, and that fact wouldn't change simply because they weren't working together. And S-24's brief record was not unimpressive. Acccording to what information Nora had at hand, the former Tony Minelli had performed well while helping to get himself and his other teammates out of some tight scrapes. "I've got to stop worrying," she told herself.

"I'd say that's a wise decision." A friendly voice startled Nora, who turned quickly around to see Dr. Francis Higgins standing just inside the door of the laboratory.

"I don't usually talk to myself, doctor," Nora returned, flashing her colleague a self-conscious smile.

"Well, you won't have much of a chance to do that with me around. I talk to myself nonstop, and I'm afraid you'll be hard pressed to get a word in edgewise!" Higgins placed a stack of notebooks on an empty section of countertop and sat his rather stocky frame down on the nearest available stool, directly across from Nora.

Nora reached over the counter and extended

her hand. "I have to tell you, I am very excited to be able to work with you, Dr. Higgins. I'm told you're close to a breakthrough in brain transplant reversal."

"I'm told that makes two of us," Higgins said warmly, clasping the proferred hand tightly. "And your oxcitoment is shared. I've heard so much about you — all of it fascinating. But I never dreamed we'd be working together."

"Nor did I. At another time and for another reason, this work would have been everything I could ever have hoped for in life — careerwise, of course," Nora quickly qualified her remark.

The gray haired, balding doctor stared hard at his new partner. Higgins looked much older than his fifty-eight years, and his body felt the effects of years of hard wear through which he required it to perform on a relentless basis. For many years he had devoted his life strictly to medical research. Before the invasion he had pushed himself relentlessly in search of a cure for cancer. After the xenoborgs came down, priorities changed; he took refuge in the New Orleans CC base, quickly familiarized himself with the work that was being done there, and for the last several months had been engrossed in trying to discover how to reinstall a Cyborg Commando's organic brain inside the cranium from which it had been taken.

He had always been wrapped up in his work, whatever it was. He had never married and, as far as he knew, had never fathered a child. Any former relationships had either been professional, platonic, or fleeting. Now he thought he recognized some of his own personality behind Nora Whitaker's eyes, in the way she moved, and in the words she was trying so carefully to choose. He felt an immediate sense of kinship. Whatever the outcome of this particular assignment, he had a feeling that it would be the last one Nora Whitaker and Frank Higgins would choose to work on. He may have many years on this woman, but she was just as ready for a rest as he was.

Higgins sighed and shook his head. "This isn't exactly what I thought I'd spend the rest of my life working toward either, but I can't think of a better cause — not to mention a more significant scientific achievement."

"You're right, of course," Nora said quietly, feeling a little embarrassed that his attitude seemed to be better adjusted than hers. Recovering quickly, and conjuring up some of the old enthusiasm she had once possessed as a part of her nature, she asked, almost exuberantly, "So what are we waiting for?"

"A last hurrah for two tired professionals?" Higgins's depth of perception temporarily threw Nora off guard.

"Maybe," she said quietly, giving the man an appreciative grin. And then, her eyes warming as she thought of John and Cris, she added, "And maybe not. Maybe this professional doesn't know how to quit, as much as she might like to."

Higgins allowed a slight, wry grin to play its way across his face, but otherwise let the comment pass.

* * *

The team of Whitaker and Higgins spent the next day or so poring over each other's logs and data books, each hoping to find one minute thread of information that he or she did not yet have, or striving to make some heretofore unrecognized conncotion botwoen two seemingly unrelated facts. But as the hours ticked away, often with no recognition from either scientist, it became painfully clear that both had already fit the same pieces of the puzzle together, leaving identical holes that had yet to be filled. It was a tired and rather disappointed duo that reported its initial findings to General Harrison and his staff.

Frank Higgins began the oral report. "Nora and I had very much hoped that combining our knowledge would lead us to a quick discovery of how to go about reuniting a brain with its body. But all we have found is that we have both come up with the same conclusions and are still unable to get over the last hurdle."

Almost as if on cue, Nora picked up where Higgins stopped. "We both know that the spinal cord, which is severed just below the medulla oblongata during the transplant operation, would be tricky to reconnect, to say the least. But it is possible, and we think we have worked out the safest and most efficient technique. We also are quite confident that nerves connected to the head, such as the optic and otic, which are rerouted to the interface and the internal computer, could be rerouted back to the organic brain capsule. The pituitary gland, pineal body, thalamus, and hypothalamus are all left in place during the operation and transplanted with the brain and, therefore, would cause no major problems. But, as Frank said, there is a major stumbling block that has both of us baffled."

She paused and took a sip of coffee out of the cup that rested on the desk in front of her before continuing.

"During the transplant surgery the human brain is placed inside a plastic shell, which is then inserted into the cyborg's brain capsule. Part of that shell is very nearly identical to the human cranium, and each one is custom-built for the brain that occupies it. This shell is lined with a colloidal substance that needs no sustenance, since it performs all of the functions of the fibrous dura mater, the arachnoid membrane, the pia mater, and the cerebral spinal fluid. Those are removed during the surgical procedure, and there is no way to preserve or reuse them. What we need to come up with is a synthetic replacement for these membranes and fluids. And this is no easy task, since we have no way of knowing what the brain will accept."

"In simple terms, we have to figure out how to fool the brain into thinking it's back in its normal environment." Higgins concluded. Then both he and Nora waited for the questions they knew were bound to come.

"And what is stopping you from beginning on that immediately?" General Garrison asked.

Nora and Frank exchanged knowing looks, and it was Nora who answered. "We have both tried experimenting on any number of living species. We have had some success in reversing the procedure in the rhesus monkey. But because we can't actually communicate with animals, because they can't verbalize how they feel or what they're thinking — or how they're thinking — we have no way of knowing how close we've come to duplicating the necessary fluids."

"But you have subjects that have lived through the reversal?"

"Yes — and no." Nora looked at Higgins, as if to ask for help.

"What Nora is trying to say is that a few of the animals have survived the procedure, but we have observed what seems to be a drastic change in behavior — personality, if you will. And a few have died within days after an apparently successful reversal. We suspect that the same synthetic material used on these animals may not be compatible

139

with the human organism, and we are at a stand-
still until we can find an answer to that question."

"But how can you know whether or not the human brain will reject these man-made membranes
unless you actually perform the operation on a
human?" Major Williams asked, and then blushed,
realizing that the question had only one obvious
answer.

Nora and Frank silently waited for General Garrison to make some kind of a comment. The man's
face looked tired and careworn. Garrison wasn't
sure how long it would be before a replacement
would be needed to carry on his duties. All he did
know for sure was that he was almost at a point of
complete mental and physical exhaustion. He
picked up the written report lying on the desk in
front of him and handed it to Captain Britton, who
stood beside his desk. The captain took it, apparently knowing without being told that the general
expected him to see that it was filed in its appropriate place. Then Garrison addressed Nora and
Frank. "Are you asking me to authorize experimen-
tal operations on human beings?" The blunt question sounded harsh when verbalized.

"We're not asking, general. We're telling you
there is no other way," Nora said quietly.

"And this synthetic substance — how long do
you think it will take to adjust it once you do proceed with testing its effectiveness?"

Frank Higgins took a deep breath and then said,

"We have no way of knowing when — or if — we will be able to successfully turn the cyborg back into the man until we have performed at least one operation — and maybe many, many more than that. Even if the first one succeeds, we still will not know for certain whether or not each individual will need a different amount or mixture of synthetic material. Until we have performed a number of successful experiments, we will not know if these cyborgs will ever be able to function inside their former human bodies."

"But in order to realize success, you must first get past the failures — isn't that correct, doctors?" The general's question was not one that Nora or Frank thought required an answer. After a brief pause Garrison continued. "Which means that there will almost certainly be a loss of lives, at least in the beginning. And for what? Exactly what do I tell prospective guinea pigs this time, doctors? And who the hell do you know who would be fool enough to go first?"

The silence that followed his question pervaded the small, overcrowded room for a few seconds. Then the videocommunicator beeped sharply, attracting everyone's attention. Nora almost leaped from her seat as a message appeared on the screen. It was an internal communique from C-12 — John had returned! And, as she would find out soon, he had brought back with him just what the doctors had ordered.

12

Except for the water that continued to flow gently out of and away from its body, the xenoborg seemed lifeless. Even the tentacles around its snout, which had twitched reflexively during the first stage of its shape-changing process, were now inert.

This would be the best time for Tony to show himself and for he and Cris to escape the area without causing a direct conflict or some kind of general alert. Cris was getting more anxious and more nervous with each passing minute. Tony had been underground for slightly more than half an hour now, and if he didn't come back up in the next few minutes Cris would have to assume the worst, and leave. . . .

. . . Or would he do that? Maybe Tony's in trouble and needs my help, Cris told himself. Maybe there's something I could do. I could blast a big enough hole to get down into that tunnel myself. I could find him and get him out.

No. . . . The logical side of Cris's mind squashed that thought as quickly as it had developed. If I did blast the hole open, I'd probably attract every monster for a mile around, not to mention the teleborg, and then neither one of us would live to fight another day.

Sometimes you have to accept death as a fact of life, he tried to convince himself. Cris Holman had endured the loss of his parents, his little sister, and the woman he loved. Now, if he had to, he would also learn to live without one of the two best friends he had ever known— a friend who, until just hours ago, he had never expected to see again.

Cris was all but resigned to abandoning his position and sneaking off so that he could make his way back to headquarters. He would wait until the one-hour absolute deadline had passed, maybe even a few minutes beyond that — Who would ever know if I pushed the limit just a little bit? — but then he would have to give up. He would have to travel slowly and do a lot of criss-crossing to keep from being seen, and if he didn't get well away from the teleborg before dawn started to break, he'd have a hell of a time keeping his presence a secret any longer than that.

"Come on, pal," he muttered. Get your better half out of that hole right now, or—"

What was that?

Cris thought he saw a dull gleam coming from some object that had jutted out of the manhole for an instant. His immediate impression was that his eyes were playing tricks on him — but just as quickly, he realized that these eyes didn't play tricks. If they saw something, then it was there.

He waited a few seconds, careful to keep the leg-lasers trained on the soggy, shrinking xeno-borg. In those few seconds, a flurry of questions and thoughts ran through his mind.

Was it Tony he had seen? It almost had to be him . . . but then again, how did he know that other people — other things — weren't also down in the tunnel? Maybe it was a man wearing a helmet, or maybe it was some kind of miniature, armored xenoborg. Anything was possible; still, he had to be hopeful and play the odds — and Tony was the most likely possibility.

Okay, if it was Tony, then why didn't he just hoist himself out of the hole and make himself visible so Cris could be sure? He knew that Cris wouldn't just be sitting on the curb waiting for him, but would be in hiding somewhere nearby, and Cris wouldn't come out of seclusion until he was positive that Tony had returned.

Well, maybe Tony didn't know as much about xenoborgs as Cris did. Maybe he wouldn't be able

145

to realize, especially on the basis of one quick glance, that the creature plopped down next to the hole was probably harmless at the moment. Or maybe he did know all that, especially the part about "*probably* harmless," and wasn't willing to risk having the xenoborg surge to life, yank out a weapon, and blow S-24's head off.

What would I do? Cris asked himself — and that was the key. Once he started imagining how he would handle the situation if his and Tony's roles were reversed, he had no trouble deciding how to proceed. It was time for P-17 to take an active part in helping this mission to succeed.

Cris pushed himself into a standing position, careful to keep the leg-lasers from bumping or scraping against something. He wanted to move quickly, to burst out through the window frame in front of him and run to the open manhole. But silence was still vitally important, so he forced himself to be deliberate. He retraced the path he had taken when he entered the building, heading for the front door, and hoped that nothing would happen for the few seconds that the manhole and the xenoborg were out of his sight.

He eased himself through the door frame, finding the opening much more difficult to negotiate this time, with the leg-lasers mounted on his shoulders. As soon as he was through it, he brought the lasers to bear on the xenoborg once again and took a second to survey the scene before him. The creature's body was still losing water, and from this angle he could see that some of the liquid was running across the street and dripping into the manhole. Would that be a clue for Tony, or would it only serve to confuse him? Only one way to find out. . . .

Cris headed straight for the hole at a fast walk, making his strides as long as he dared. He pivoted his upper body slightly as he moved, to keep the leg-lasers fixed on the monster, and held his thumbs poised a half-inch away from the fire buttons. If the thing moved at all, he would drill it with a pair of beams and deal with the consequences afterward.

He stopped about three feet in front of the hole and about six feet away from the left rear flank of the xenoborg. From this close, he could hear the water dripping and gently splashing as it cascaded over the edge of the hole and down across the rungs of the ladder. He stepped closer to the hole and bent over to look inside it — and, suddenly, he could see light coming from inside the tunnel!

For a second, a burst of dim illumination washed over the wall of the manhole, coming up to within a few feet of street level. Then the hole was dark again, and after about three seconds another flash appeared. It was a signal — and it could only be coming from S-24.

Trying to keep one eye on the xenoborg and one eye directed into the depths of the manhole,

Cris knelt down facing the hole with his thighs perpendicular to the street. The next time he saw a flash of light from below, he flicked on the lamps in his upper legs for just an instant. Most of the illumination went out across the street, but he hoped that enough of it would get into the hole so that Tony would know his signal was being returned.

It worked. As Cris peered down into the manhole, another flash of light came from below. This time Cris could see S-24's head and shoulders outlined by the illumination from Tony's throat-light. Tony lifted his head toward the sky, raised one arm with a finger extended as if to say "Just a minute," and then began coming up the ladder hand over hand.

Seconds later, P-17 and S-24 were reunited. As Tony brought his head above the surface of the street once again, he looked in the direction of the inert xenoborg. Cris tapped him lightly on the top of his head to get his attention, then motioned for him to hurry.

Tony didn't need to be told twice. He pulled his truncated body out of the hole and began scrambling across the pavement directly away from where the creature lay. Cris got to his feet and followed, using short strides to keep from getting too far ahead of his friend. When they were both a couple of hundred feet away from the hole, they ducked around the corner of a building and stopped. Tony, true to form, was the first to speak.

"Am I glad to see you!" he breathed, looking up at the Cyborg Commando who towered over him.

"Same here," Cris whispered. "Did you drop the stuff?"

"Oh, yeah — right where it'll do the most good."

"Okay. Now let's get you put back together and get the hell out of here." Cris lifted the leg-lasers off his shoulders, unlocked the knee joints — which also deactivated the weapons — and set the mechanism on the ground so that Tony could reattach his torso to his hips.

"What is that thing doing sitting there?" Tony asked as he maneuvered himself into position.

"Just sitting, as far as I can tell," Cris said. "It's trying to shrink so it can get into the hole—"

"And while it's changing shape, it can't do anything else," Tony interrupted. "Jeez, I should have known."

"I thought I saw you stick your head up once—"

"Yeah, but I panicked. I figured you were staying away to keep from being found, and I thought the thing was waiting for me to come up."

"So . . ."

"So I stayed at the bottom of the hole and did the only thing I could think of — flashed my light on and off every once in a while, so that maybe you'd see it and know I was waiting for help."

"I did see it, but not until I got right next to the hole. It wasn't bright enough—"

"And neither was I," Tony said, punctuating the

149

remark with two clicks as the latches holding his hips to his torso were closed and locked. "I should have come part way up the ladder to be sure the light would carry high enough."

"None of that matters," Cris said, taking S-24 by the arm and helping him get to his feet. "We got the job done — actually, *you* got the job done — and, as my old friend John always says, it's the end result that matters."

"Yeah, well, the end result remains to be seen — and we're not out of the woods yet, if you get my meaning," Tony said, glancing around at the steel and concrete structures that surrounded them.

"Right. . . . But there's one more thing I have to do before we head out. Back me up, okay?" Cris came out from behind the corner of the building and started to walk back toward the xenoborg.

"Cris, where the hell . . . ?"

"Take it easy. We can afford another couple of minutes. And this is one part of this mission I think you'll like."

Tony shrugged. "I hope you know what you're doing," he said, trying hard not to let his skepticism get the best of him. He followed several yards behind as Cris strode back to the manhole, stepped around it, and stood directly in front of the inert creature that was still oozing and slowly becoming smaller. About forty-five minutes had passed since the creature had begun to expel liquid, and it was now down to about half of its original bulk. In another few minutes, Cris figured, it would stop throwing off water and begin to elongate so that it could get into the manhole — but by then it wouldn't matter.

"This is for dad and Lois," Cris growled under his breath. He brought his right foot up and out to the side, then swung it in a flat arc that smacked the xenoborg right in the snout. A few large chunks of flesh went flying, and a couple of the thing's tentacles dropped to the pavement. "And for Sara," he added. "And for Maura." Twice more his foot went into and through the soft flesh, hitting the thing with ten times more force than a human bo ing could have mustered. He suddenly didn't care about the noise he was making or the extra time he was taking — all that mattered was beating this mindless mound of flesh into a pulp.

After the third blow, the xenoborg's snout was almost disintegrated. The thing might survive, but when it regained awareness it might be able to remember what had happened — and maybe it would spread the word to its "friends" that parking in front of an open manhole is not a good idea.

Cris stared at the mangled snout for a couple of seconds, suppressing the urge to keep hammering away at the thing until it was spread all over the street. Then he turned away and went back to where Tony had stood watching his display of rage.

"Hey, pal, did that feel good?" Tony asked, feeling a combination of sympathy and concern for his partner.

Cris just looked back at the mess he had left and sadly shook his head. "I've wanted to do that for such a long time now. . . . But to answer your question, no — and you know what's really scary? I'm not sure anything will ever feel good again."

"I know exactly how you feel, pal," Tony said quietly. He took hold of Cris's arm and steered him away from the grisly sight. "C'mon, let's get the hell out of here."

* * *

It took two hours for P-17 and S-24 to get five miles away from the manhole, to a place far enough away from the teleborg that the concentration of xenoborgs was relatively light. Twice they had to take cover and remain hidden for several minutes to avoid being discovered by small bands of monsters that were apparently foraging. Finally, instead of being inside the area where they would be looked upon as intruders and threats to the teleborg, they were back in fairly safe territory — where Cris and Tony figured that any xenoborgs they ran across would rather avoid them than take them on.

And now, for the first time since the mission had

started, they were on their own — free to seek out and destroy any monsters they could flush out while making their way back to the Manitowoc base. Their mission had been important, and it was satisfying to have pulled it off, but this was going to be the fun part.

"We have about an hour before the base is expecting to hear from us," Cris said. "Time enough to do some hunting."

"Yes, *sir*, lieutenant!" Tony said, rubbing his palms together.

"Let's head for that high ground off to the northeast and see what we can rustle up."

Now that they didn't have to stay hidden and could use all of their electronic senses without worrying about being detected, it would be simple to locate any targets that might be in the area. Cris and Tony moved about two hundred yards apart and advanced toward the northeast through a lightly wooded area, using their radios to keep track of each other's location and to communicate. At the same time, they scanned the area in front of them with their infrared sensors and kept their "ears" sharp for any evidence of radio signals other than their own.

"Veer toward that clump of trees on the slope off to my right," said Cris. "I have a hunch."

"Yep," said Tony, angling his path and his sensors in that direction. "There's something big and warm among those trees — more than one some-

thing, from the looks of it — and I'd say it's probably not a family of elephants."

Cris moved to one side of the grove and shuffled back and forth within an area of a few square
yards while he waited for Tony to get into position
about fifty yards to his left. He had to assume that
their radio conversations had been detected by
now, and if he stood still and talked at the same
time he would enable any xenoborgs with sensors
to get a good idea of his location, so he had to
keep moving even though he was essentially staying in the same place.

Just as Cris was about to give the order for
Tony to move closer, a radio transmission burst
out of the trees. He and Tony picked up the signal
immediately, and even though they couldn't deci-
pher it, they had a pretty good idea what it was.

"Sounds like the boss is calling for help," Cris
said.

"Well, shall we turn the heat on, lieutenant?"

"After you, corporal."

Tony moved a few yards closer to the edge of
the clump of trees. From this vantage point he
could make out four or five distinct heat-shapes, all
of them pivoting sluggishly as they tried to hide
behind trees and keep themselves out of Tony's
line of fire. The strategy was about as ludicrous,
and as successful, as a hippopotamus concealing
itself behind a sapling.

Tony targeted on the largest one first, knowing it

would be the leader and the one most likely to be equipped with technological weaponry. He stopped, raised his arms, and locked his knuckles into the firing position. This moment was the most dangerous second or two of any combat encounter; while Tony was stationary, he would be a sitting duck for a laser blast, a rocket, or any other kind of weapon that a monster might be able to fire. But he had two things going for him: a xenoborg could only aim at something it could see, and the monsters didn't have sophisticated internal computers to help them direct their weapons, so their first shot — even if they could get one off — was usually not on target. In the darkness, and with their vision obscured by the same trees they were trying to hide behind, Tony guessed that he would be able to start blasting away before they knew exactly where the attack was coming from.

He guessed right, with about a second to spare.

Twin beams shot out of Tony's knuckles, each searing a path across the near flank of the largest shape. The monster jerked reflexively away from the source of the blasts, and in the next instant a return beam of laser fire shot into the air, sizzling in a line that sheared off a couple of low branches and crackled through the air about thirty feet above Tony's head. If the monster had not been wounded just before its laser went off, the lucky shot would have burned a hole right through S-24's chest — and Tony Minelli's brain.

Before the thing could recover and bring its weapon to bear once more, Tony darted a few feet to his left, threw himself down to a prone position, and fired again. This time he left the lasers on for a little more than one-tenth of a second — long enough for them to burn a pair of diagonal wounds all the way through the creature's hindquarters.

That was all the xenoborg could take. Still sending out its radio message, probably by means of some sort of automatic transmitter, it began to shuffle frantically away from the source of the laser blasts while its own weapon flashed intermittently, sending out harmless bursts of light in random directions. The monster closest to the big one also began to move away from Tony, as though the panic of its leader was infectious. Chuckling softly, Tony gave the creature time to turn and start running away. Then he fired a pair of blasts that hit the thing in the rear and, a split-second later, popped out the front of its body and lit the sky in front of the thing like twin searchlights.

Three more creatures were still huddled behind the trees where they had originally taken cover, either too scared or too stupid to try doing anything else. Tony let the first two go and turned his attention to the others. Judging by their size and their reluctance to meet him head-on, he figured they were ordinary monsters — the kind that could only attack if he got in reach of their pincers or tentacles. He could have walked up to within twenty feet of them and blasted them at point-blank range, but a more original idea occurred to him.

"Keep your fire parallel to the ground, pal," Tony radioed to Cris. "I'm going up."

"You're going *where*? Oh, no—"

By the time Cris started to object, Tony had already picked out a tree at the edge of the grove that looked strong enough to hold him, clambered up the trunk, locked his legs around a thick lower branch, and aimed his lasers at a dead tree about ten feet away from where one of the xenoborgs was "hiding." Using a single beam and aiming it to slice through the tree at a downward angle, he chopped off the two-foot-diameter trunk about five feet above the ground. The tree toppled in the direction of the slanted cut and came down across the monster's body.

The thing's tough outer surface made a crunching, splintering sound as the tree broke through it, and before the xenoborg could react, the tree had hit the ground, virtually cutting the monster in half in the process. Sprays of liquid and small globs of flesh went flying in all directions away from the tree, and the front part of the monster's body reared up in a futile attempt to get away from the massive cylinder of wood that had crushed it and was half-pinning it to the ground.

The crash the tree made when it hit was enough to send the other two xenoborgs running for their lives — or, at least, that's what they tried to do.

Before they could even get fully turned around to head back up the slope the way they had come, Tony turned his lasers on each of them in turn. Using four sweeping blasts on each creature, he sectioned them into still-living but helpless mounds of flesh that could do no more than flail their tentacles and push their spindly legs ineffectually against the ground.

Cris watched Tony's pyrotechnic display out of the corner of his eye as he waited for his chance to make little pieces out of big xenoborgs. Tony's first blasts had been designed to send the leader and its one companion running out of the trees on a route that would take them directly across Cris's line of fire.

Since the leader had stopped firing once it sensed it was out of danger, Cris waited until both of them were well clear of the trees, imagining how they must be feeling more secure with each passing second. Then he got off a single, short laser blast that led the larger xenoborg by several feet — designed not to hit it, but to make it stop and turn. The thing came to an immediate halt and instinctively curled its snout back toward where the laser blast had come from. That motion gave Cris the target he was hoping for.

Using the same tactic he had employed to disable and then destroy dozens of monsters just like this one, Cris's next blast cut down and through the creature's snout — shearing off most of its tentacles, including the one that was holding its laser. Then, thanks to his infrared sensors, he detected a couple of spots along the leader's flank that were not radiating heat. He had seen this sort of thing before — grenade launchers that could be extruded from "portholes" along the monster's side — and he know just what to do.

His next pair of laser beams cut a swath along the monster's length, parallel to the ground. Before the projectile weapons could be aimed and fired, P-17's lasers found the places inside the xenoborg's body where its explosive grenades were stored. He only actually hit a couple of the grenades, but that was enough.

When one exploded from contact with the laser, it set off all the others around it so rapidly that the successive explosions sounded like one continuous boom. The monster erupted like a miniature volcano, its remains spraying fifty or sixty feet in every direction, and the concussion was so strong that Cris, standing seventy-five yards away, was almost knocked off his feet.

When he stabilized himself again a couple of seconds later, the first thing Cris noticed was the absence of the insistent radio signal that the thing had been sending out for the last several minutes. Then he saw that behind what was left of the leader, the smaller xenoborg had been toppled on its side by the force of the blast. It was teetering back and forth on its flank, legs churning comically in the air as it tried to right itself. It might have been able to succeed, but the side of its body facing up was gouged in several places. The grenade launchers and other hardware the leader was carrying inside its body had been turned into lethal projectiles themselves, and some of the metal fragments had been driven into the other creature's body.

"Cris! Are you okay?"

"Yeah. No problem."

"No problem? Even from way over here, that blast really shook my tree! What did you do?"

"It was carrying grenades, and—"

"Say no more. I just wish you had waited until I had both feet back on terra firma."

"Sorry. I guess I'm just not used to working with monkeys."

"But it worked! You should have seen that big ugly bug when the tree fell on his miserable body. First time I ever got one by clubbing it — and what a club!"

"It *was* a pretty awesome sight at that," Cris agreed happily, and then added sternly, "but don't go off on any more tangents, okay, corporal? I'm responsible for you and your actions, you know, and I don't need you to get me in trouble."

"No, I imagine you can do that without my help," Tony chuckled and then he and Cris both burst into laughter.

"Hell, I give up on trying to elicit from you the respect my position deserves," Cris said, extending his mechanical upper limbs toward the sky in a gesture of surrender.

"If you ask me, that's a smart move, *sir*," Tony said in mock seriousness.

"Okay smartass, let's just mop up and get going." Cris responded wearily.

Tony disposed of the three carcasses still in the grove by setting his microwave projectors on narrow beam and methodically cooking each chunk of flesh until the cell walls had broken down and the water contained within them had either boiled away or seeped into the ground. In the meantime, Cris did the same with the larger pieces of the leader's body that still remained in the area where the blast had gone off. Then he looked over at the xenoborg, wounded but still mostly intact, that was still struggling to right itself.

He stepped up to the front of the thing and eliminated its only chance of fighting back by slicing a laser beam through its snout, just behind where its tentacles began. Then he searched around until he found a good-sized piece of wood, about ten feet long and seven or eight inches in diameter. He lifted it as though it weighed no more than a baseball bat, slung it over his shoulder, and carried it back to the xenoborg.

He strolled casually around the monster for a minute or so, brandishing the log and hoping that the creature could somehow understand what was about to happen to it. Then he stopped directly in front of its truncated snout, staring directly at what looked like an eye-spot, raised the club, and brought it down across the creature's "face" as hard as he could.

Again and again he pounded on the thing, punctuating each swing with a grunt or a curse and trying to make each blow more damaging than the last. By the time Tony came out of the trees toward where Cris was standing, the front third of the xenoborg's body was a battered, shapeless, oozing pile of pulp, and the front of P-17's body was splattered with liquid and small pieces of alien flesh.

Tony had a hard time adjusting to the deliberate, brutal, almost maniacal way in which Cris was killing this monster. And it made him nervous — not because he had any feelings for the xenoborg, but because he was worried about what might be happening to Cris Holman.

He called his friend's name three times as he approached, but got no response. Then Tony got next to Cris, caught his arm on the backswing, and shouted at him.

"Cris! What's wrong?"

"Nothing," Cris said, his voice like steel. "I'm killing this one the way I'd like to kill every one of them — slowly, and painfully."

"I understand," said Tony. "But this isn't the way. You know that."

"Yeah," Cris said, already noticeably calmer

now that his tirade had been interrupted. "I know."

"C'mon, pal, we can't all go around carrying logs and trying to bash every xenoborg into its component parts. That would take forever, and we don't have—"

"I know all that," Cris interrupted, irritation in his tone. "Do you think you're talking to a rookie?"

"No. I'm talking to a friend of mine — a man — who has been storing up a lot of pain for a long time. And I'm pointing out the obvious because, right now, I'm not sure he can see it for himself."

Cris let the piece of wood fall to the ground. "You're right," he said, now subdued. "I almost lost it there."

"You *did* lose it. But the important thing is, you got it back."

"Yeah. I think maybe you showed up just in time."

"Aw, don't thank me. That's what two-piece, cybernetic, laser-knuckled friends are for. Now, we'd better toast what's left of this thing and be on our way."

"No. Leave it the way it is."

"What? After smashing part of it to pulp, you want to let the rest of it survive?"

"I want it to live, because if there's a way it can communicate what just happened to it, maybe the rest of these monsters will realize we mean business. Slicing up a xenoborg with a laser and broiling it with a microwave beam is very effective, but kind of an impersonal way to kill something. Brute force is a universal language, and I have no doubt that this thing knows exactly what I just told it. We can slice them, we can cook them, we can blast them, or we can simply beat them to bits if we care to. One way or another, we *are* going to beat them — and it's about time they started to realize that."

"Well," Tony said, "I'm not going to worry about you any more. Seems like your head is screwed on as straight as it could be."

"Actually, it's held in place by welds."

"You know what I—"

"Yeah, I know what you meant." P-17 rested a hand on S-24's shoulder. "Come on, let's go."

* * *

After moving for fifteen minutes at a slow trot, Cris and Tony reached the top of the ridge they had been heading toward. It seemed to be the highest spot for miles around, and a good place for them to send out a radio signal pointed toward Manitowoc.

Cris, as the ranking member of the team, would send the transmission — not a message as such, but simply a two-second burst of coded pulses that would summarize how the mission had gone and, by implication, tell the strategic planners back at the base what their next move should be. The information had to be passed as quickly as possible to prevent any xenoborg sensors from detecting the transmission and possibly tracing its route.

For all the months since the invasion, the xenoborgs had been kept ignorant of the exact location of the Manitowoc base, for two reasons. First, every Cyborg Commando that operated out of that base — or any other one, for that matter — knew that the worst thing he or she could do would be to betray the whereabouts of headquarters. No one ever entered or exited an accessway before being sure that the movement was unobserved — not only by xenoborgs, but by humans who might unwittingly give away the information. At the Manitowoc base alone, three CCs had stayed aboveground until their primary batteries were drained rather than risk being discovered while they made their way to and through an accessway. They were all later rescued and recharged, but they could just as easily have died — and they would have been willing to, rather than reveal the disguised passageway that led to their underground quarters.

Second, no primary base ever transmitted or received radio signals on the same frequency for any longer than two seconds. The people who staffed each base and all the CC operatives knew that some xenoborgs were equipped with communication units that could send and receive signals or track the source and destination of a foreign transmission. But they could only track on a certain frequency at one time, and they needed to monitor a specific signal for at least three to five seconds in order to get a good fix on where it was coming from and going to. Once the people in the underground bases realized this limitation of the aliens' equipment, it was a simple matter to come up with a procedure for rapid, computer-assisted frequency changes that occurred every two seconds whenever an especially long message had to be transmitted. Even if a xenoborg in the area happened to be monitoring a certain frequency when it was used for part of a message, the creature would only "hear" the signal for a short time — too short to make any use of the information.

When a CC in the field contacted headquarters, he or she never talked to another CC or a human being; the contact was always directly with a computer. By using binary language, a CC's computer-assisted transmitter could convey an enormous amount of information in a very short time — which is what Cris was about to do.

After they reached the spot from where P-17 would transmit, Cris and Tony waited in silence for about three minutes, until 0300 hours. For the purpose of getting the report on this mission, the base's homing signal and receiving equipment were only activated on the predesignated frequency for five seconds starting exactly on the hour every hour. If they had missed this opportunity to send back their report, Cris and Tony would have had to wait another hour — and if the base did not hear from them by the 0500 reporting window, they would be presumed disabled or lost in action.

But all of that was academic now. Cris had decided on the proper message to send, it had been translated into "computer code" by his electronic brain, and now that same brain was about to take over and make sure the information got through.

At 0259:55, Cris oriented P-17's body in the general direction of the Manitowoc base, roughly north-northeast of where he stood. At 0300, P-17's computer took control. When it detected receipt of the homing signal, it made a microscopic adjustment in the alignment of P-17's transmitter so that the signal going out would travel precisely the same path that the homing beacon had taken to reach Cris. Then the news traveled almost instantaneously from a hilltop outside Milwaukee to a super-sensitive antenna sixty-five miles away.

Cris's message, distilled to its essentials by the unenthusiastic, impersonal computer, went something like this: "We did it!" (Mission accomplished.) "Tony got in and dumped all the stuff!" (S-24 completed incursion and egress.) "It took a while to get out, but we blasted a few along the way!" (Minor delays and minimal resistance along escape route.) "And the stupid teleborg doesn't have any idea what we did to it!" (Secrecy was not compromised.) "See you in a few hours! Give it one right down the throat for me and Tony, will you?" (Estimated return to base by 0730. Out.)

At 0300:03, the internal computer finished sending the message, shut off the transmitter, and simultaneously returned control for all of P-17's non-autonomous operations to Cris Holman's brain.

"That's that," Cris said to Tony.

"Well, so much for the fine art of verbal communication," Tony said. "I wish every politician's speech I had ever heard lasted as long as that."

"And I wish any single speech I'd ever heard had as much substance," Cris said.

"We did it, didn't we?" Tony's voice suddenly turned soft and serious.

"Yeah, we did it." Cris answered, equally somber. "Now let's just hope it was worth the risk."

"Risk?" Tony was abruptly effervescent again. "What risks did *you* take? Lemme tell you how much fun it was going on a Thursday morning stroll — without legs! — through a dark, filthy concrete tunnel full of tentacles and dead people and—"

"Slow down, corporal." Cris started walking down the slope toward home, and Tony fell into step right beside him. "We have a lot of ground to cover and a few hours to spend doing it. So take it from the top, and take your time."

"Okay. . . .You shoulda seen it! When I dropped the food, the thing went absolutely crazy—"

"I thought you were going to take it from the top."

"Aw, come on. This is the really *good* part. . . ."

13

April 24, 2036

". . . And instead of looking out at your nonsmiling face, the first thing I saw was the blind side of a xenoborg. Imagine my surprise, followed quickly by my silent shriek of terror, followed by my three-rungs-at-once descent of the ladder, followed—"

"I think I know the rest," said Cris. "Thank you, corporal, for that mildly entertaining and absolutely chaotic description of what you did to kill time while I was babysitting with your lower body in the middle of xenoborg country. And it's a good thing for you that I didn't run into any big trouble while you were traipsing around underground, because if I had been forced to fight—"

"Okay, okay. So I concede that your part in this drama was an important one. As the supporting character—"

"Give me a break!" Cris interrupted. He couldn't begin to express how happy he was to have Tony back by his side. At the same time, a small part of him — the part that thought of himself as Lieutenant P-17 — did not appreciate getting backtalk from a corporal. And he was a little uncomfortable with the way he and Tony communicated, because he was worried about being reprimanded when his superiors back at the base reviewed the computer tapes of what they had said and done during this mission. Things had not always been done by the book, to put it mildly — and P-17, as the CC in charge, was responsible for S-24's deviations from standard procedure as well as his own.

But a much larger part — the person and the personality of Cris Holman that would always be inside his organic brain — didn't care about all the military policies and regulations. They got the job done, so even if they weren't model soldiers, what difference did it make? The people who decided to team them up for this mission knew that Cris and Tony had been fast friends in their previous lives, so from that standpoint they should have expected what they got. You just don't pull rank on a friend.

Suddenly a silent alarm went off inside P-17's internal computer. Cris had instructed his electronic brain to alert him shortly before 0600, so that he and Tony could find out if their subterfuge had succeeded. "It's almost time," Cris said. "Turn to the south and get ready."

Both of them faced the direction they had come from. The western sky, to their right, was still dark, and along the eastern horizon the dawn of a new day was beginning to break. In between, to the south and slightly west, the sky was a medium-dark gray, the line dividing ground and air just barely discernible to vision in the normal spectrum.

P-17 and S-24 activated their infrared sensors and gradually turned up their audio sensors to maximum sensitivity. As they did so, they filtered out sounds they didn't care about — the chirping of songbirds, the scratching of a squirrel's claws on the trunk of a tree, the rustling of last autumn's fallen leaves being pushed around by the gentle morning breeze, the whooshing movement of the air itself — until they could hear nothing at all.

Then, from far in the distance to the south, they started to pick up the sounds they were hoping to hear: the whine of jet engines struggling to keep their planes aloft at low altitudes, the shriek of missiles cutting through the air at almost the speed of sound. They saw minuscule spots of heat growing larger and closer — the planes and projectiles approaching their target.

And a moment later came the most welcome sights and sounds of all. First, flashes of heat that all emanated from the same spot, somewhere just beyond the horizon, and made the cool early-morning air take on a pinkish-orange glow. Then, the reverberating, muffled booms of dozens of

171

massive explosions all taking place within a few seconds of each other. Cris thought he also felt the ground vibrate, but then he realized that his knees were actually shaking as the electrical impulses sent out by his excited organic brain found their way into his extremities.

All the commotion came from the teleborg that had been the object of the mission. The scientists had estimated that roughly six hours after Tony dropped off the super-rich food capsules, the massive alien would have had time to take in the nutrients and virtually every cell in its body would be blindly absorbed in assimilating and processing the best meal the thing had probably ever eaten. The cells normally devoted to receiving sensory input and manipulating the teleborg's weaponry would join in the feast, at least so that they would only respond sluggishly, if at all — and this would be the ideal time to launch an all-out attack on the monster.

Judging from the intensity of the heat and sonic vibrations that P-17 and S-24 had been able to pick up from dozens of miles away, most of the bombs and missiles had found their target — and that meant the mission was a success. Two Cyborg Commandos had done the job they were entrusted with, and because of their effort man's conventional weapons could finally be brought to bear against the largest and most formidable of the alien invaders. The Cyborg Commando Force and the rest of mankind had finally come up with a way to merge their resources into a two-fisted assault that could kill a teleborg.

The significance of that observation was not lost on Cris Holman as he stared for another few seconds at the radiance in the southern sky. He motioned for Tony to turn his audio and visual sensors back to normal, did the same, and then said softly, "I think this could be the turning point."

"I was thinking more or less the same thing," Tony responded with calm seriousness. "If we can do this to one of them, we can do it to all of them. And . . ."

Tony wasn't quite sure how to end that thought, but Cris had a response ready. "And we'll prove to these . . . aliens . . . that picking on the human race was a very bad idea, and all the bugs will give up and go back where they came from."

"Or," Tony chimed in, "maybe we can develop some delicious 'xenoborg vitamins' and do the same thing to every one of those creatures that we just did to the teleborg."

Cris was not to be outdone. "Or better yet, we can come up with some kind of insecticide that doesn't hurt people but makes xenoborgs drop in their tracks."

All of a sudden, the world was teeming with new possibilities, with hope that had not existed a few hours ago. By the time P-17 and S-24 reached the outskirts of Manitowoc, the sun had risen well above the eastern horizon, and the new day seemed especially bright.

* * *

Nora was waiting for them when Cris and Tony cleared the accessway and stepped into the debriefing room. Tony saw nothing in her face but unbridled happiness, but Cris thought he detected something else in his mother's eyes.

She tried to hug them at the same time and they returned the gesture, surrounding and enveloping her for a moment. "I can't tell you how glad I was to hear that your message had come through," she said to Cris.

"I think you just did," Cris said appreciatively. "I wish you'd try to stop worrying about me so much," he added.

"I've told you before," Nora said with a tinge of irritation. "The day I see my whole son standing in front of me again is the day I'll stop worrying. Until then—"

"It was really pretty easy," Tony said, sending the conversation in a different direction. "In fact, I'd say there was never a time when we were in any real danger. Isn't that right, sir?"

"Yes, corporal. I was just about to make that point myself."

"Oh, stop it, you two," Nora said, half-smiling. "Anything you say now may be held against you after I have a chance to review the tapes, so don't try pulling my leg."

"Gosh, we'd never do that to you," Tony said. "I've had it done to me a few times, and I can tell you it's really not much fun."

"But it is a good way of cutting you down to size," Cris said.

"Oh, yeah?" For once he was at a loss for words, and that was as much of a retort as Tony could manage before two technicians accosted him and began leading him over to the socket where his computer would be plugged in for debriefing. Cris knew they would be back for him in a minute or so, but he had time for one more important question.

"Is John okay?" he asked his mother softly, when Tony was out of earshot.

"Yes, thank God. He got back a few hours ago. He had a tough time, and we lost someone else, but John came through all right. He's a survivor, Cris. You should know that by now."

"Yeah. And he taught me everything he knows — which is why I wish you wouldn't worry so much."

"I can't help it, Cris. And you should also know that by now."

"Okay," he murmured, reaching out to touch her shoulder as the technicians came up behind him.

Nora spoke loudly enough for both Cris and Tony to hear. "Why don't you two come to my quarters after downloading your mission tapes and give me the informal version?"

"Sure, mom," Cris said. "But I think you'll discover later that the informal version is already on record anyway — at least, Tony's part of it."

"And a thrilling story it is indeed," Tony said, not missing a beat.

"I can hardly wait," she said as she turned to leave the room. "See you soon."

Fifteen minutes later, Cris and Tony had finished feeding the computer records of their mission into the base's information bank. Two hours after that, they left Nora's quarters after filling her in on how things had gone and enjoying some casual conversation. By then, she was ready for sleep — she had not rested in almost twenty-four hours — and P-17 and S-24 were due for recharging and a sleep period of their own. Both of them were pleased to find out that they were again being allowed to bunk together in the room that Cris had formerly occupied by himself.

Just before they settled down, Cris voiced a thought that had been gnawing at the back of his mind for some time. "Did you notice anything . . . unusual . . . about my mother, Tony?"

"Hmm. She was affectionate, overprotective, just a wee bit frosty. . . . Nope. The same Nora Whitaker I've always known. Why do you ask?"

"I can't pin it down. I just have the feeling that she knows something she's not telling us."

"She probably knows a thousand things she isn't going to tell us. She's a very smart lady."

"That's not what I mean. For instance, remember when we told her about seeing the heat and the explosions in the distance? I expected her to be real happy — that was what made the whole mission worthwhile — but she had this sort of artificial smile on her face, like she was humoring us. We did see the teleborg get blown up, didn't we?"

"Sure. She told us herself that eighty percent of the bombs and missiles got through to the target."

Suddenly, something occurred to Cris. "But she never came right out and said that the teleborg had been killed."

"That seems like the sort of thing that would go without saying. That thing may have been big and tough, but we threw enough firepower at it to flatten a small village. Come on, Cris, I think you're letting your natural pessimism run away with you again. Look on the bright side!"

"Okay," said Cris. "The bright side it is." Then, as his brain drifted into sleep, he added to himself, I just hope it doesn't turn out to be a flash in the pan. . . .

* * *

The precise dosages of sleep-inducing chemicals that had been fed into Cris's and Tony's brains ran their course in five hours, as usual, and

P-17 and S-24 awoke feeling psychologically and physically refreshed. While their brains slept, technicians monitored and replenished the fluids and nutrients that kept the organic parts of their bodies alive and healthy. And, since both of them had recharged their primary power supplies before going to sleep, their technological parts were literally brimming with energy as well. The overall effect was to make them feel, upon awakening, almost immediately energetic, enthusiastic, and ready to do whatever they were required to do next. Or, at least, it was supposed to work that way. . . .

"Uhhh . . ." groaned P-17, who, chemicals or no, found it difficult to shift his brain into high gear right after getting up. Cris Holman had never been quick to rise, and it didn't seem to make any difference that his brain was now residing in a nonhuman body.

"Aww, is the lootennint still sleepy?" Tony Minelli's brain had never had any trouble waking up, and S-24 was the same way. However, Tony did miss the pleasurable sensation of stretching and flexing his muscles for a few minutes before he hopped out of the sack. Now he had a body composed of inflexible, unstretchable mechanical muscles, and although he still went through the motions, it just wasn't the same.

"Gimme a coupla minutes," Cris mumbled, still too groggy to be argumentative.

"You'd think they'd be able to do something

about your fuzzy-headedness — adjust your dosage, let you sleep a little longer, maybe wire a couple of electrodes to your—"

"For your information, they tried." Cris paused for effect and added, "But I guess since this turned out to be my biggest fault, they decided to let me keep it."

"Aha! I knew it! All you need to get rolling in the morning, or whenever, is a couple of shots of sarcasm. I guess that makes me the world's most expensive alarm clock."

"And the most obnoxious, too."

"Hey, pal, you get what you pay for."

"And you're gonna get—"

The beep of the videocommunicator across the room distracted Cris before he could finish. Both of them knew better than to ignore the unit, since it could only be activated from outside their quarters by someone who outranked Cris. He got to his feet, went over, and pushed the "Ready to Receive" button. Instantly a message filled the center of the screen:

ITINERARY, 25-26 APRIL 2036

LT. P-17, CPL. S-24

1530: POST-MISSION EVALUATION, RM 4C

1600: R&R

1700: GROUP BRIEFING SESSION W/C-12 AND O-33, RM 1B

1800: REFIT

2000: SP6

0100: MISSION START

"Well," said Tony, "according to the clock in my chest, that means we've got about fifteen minutes to brush our teeth and comb our hair."

Cris was more interested in the third item on the list. He was going to see John again soon, and apparently the three of them were being sent on a mission together along with someone called O-33. "Wait till you meet C-12 — John to his friends," Cris said. "He's one of a kind, believe me."

"A *Cee*?" Tony echoed. "I've never even seen a Cee, much less worked with one. Are they really as slow as people say?"

"What people have you been talking to?"

"The technos in New Orleans told me that practically all of the older models were destroyed in the invasion, and the ones left around are about as useful as mosquito netting on a space station."

"Did any of them say they had actually seen a C model?"

"Now that you mention it, no."

"Then I suggest that you keep your second-hand opinions to yourself. If John Edwards hears you talking that way, you might find out real fast that you can be broken into three or four pieces instead of just two. He's a lot of things, but slow is not one of them."

It was the first time since their reunion that Cris had spoken to Tony that way, and the effect was not lost on S-24. When Tony responded, he was truly contrite.

"I'm sorry, Cris. One of these days I'm going to learn to think before I talk, at least some of the time."

"Yeah, and one of these days I'm going to learn how to fly." Now that his moment of anger had passed, Cris's tone was laden with its usual friendly sarcasm once again. He spent the next few minutes giving Tony a brief history of what he and John had done together, and then it was time for them to leave.

*   *   *

The post-mission briefing went well, all things considered. Traynor had only a few critical things to say about some of the particular ways in which Cris and Tony had bent the rules — and a couple of his observations absolutely shocked Cris.

"Of course," Traynor said, "we would have known if you had waited for S-24 longer than you were supposed to. I don't know how you expected to get away with that."

"I *thought* about it!" Cris blurted out. "But I wasn't going to do it!"

"Gee," Tony interjected. "I don't know whether to pat you on the back or bust you in the mouth."

"You did more than think about it," Traynor said. "Your voice recorder picked up a sentence — low in volume, but very distinct — that went something like, 'Who would ever know if I pushed the limit just a little bit?' If you didn't say it, then the world's best ventriloquist must have been standing right behind you."

"Jeez," Cris said, embarrassed and apprehensive. If he had said that instead of just thinking it, then what else had he verbalized without knowing it? "I didn't realize I was talking to myself. That's really dumb," he added, hoping that by chastising himself he could save Traynor the trouble of doing it.

"It's a natural thing," the man said. "But in certain circumstances, it could also be a very dumb thing to do." Traynor put a half-smile on his face, an expression that Cris hated because he never could be sure if the man knew something or if he just wanted Cris to *think* he knew something.

Cris was also gently criticized for, of all things, shaking Tony's tree. "When you set off all the grenades inside that xenoborg at one time, you endangered the safety of your partner. If he hadn't been holding onto the tree securely when the shock wave hit him, he could have fallen and been damaged. Not to mention the fact that he should never have been in that tree in the first place!" Traynor shot a scathing look in Tony's direction and then continued, addressing Cris again.

"Keeping the corporal in line is one of your responsibilities. If your superiors get wind of your casual conduct I'm sure you would be reprimanded for letting him get by with his antics, S-24 would be reprimanded for his little playground trick, and the two of you would never be assigned to the same mission team again. Is that what you want?"

"No!" The answer came from Cris and Tony simultaneously.

"All right. Now, S-24, I do have one very important point to make concerning your acrobatic act."

"Yes?" Tony's voice quavered a bit.

"It's a good thing you cut down a *dead* tree. . . ."

Cris could hardly believe his ears. Tony was actually being complimented?

". . . because if you had aimed at a live one, your internal computer would have prevented your laser from firing. And, as we found out during your sleep period, you have a faulty override relay in your right forearm."

"Which means?" Tony asked, anxious for the man to get to the point.

Traynor looked at S-24 sharply, angry at the interruption. "Which means that the energy from that firing pulse would not have been shunted and reabsorbed properly, and it is very likely that your arm would have either exploded or melted."

Tony knew that his internal computer's override mechanism would not let him intentionally target a weapon on any living thing other than an alien — including, of course, a healthy tree. But he hadn't thought about that at the time, and he could have just as easily aimed at a live one instead of the dead one he chose. The words "exploded or melted" reverberated in his mind as he sat shaking his head slowly, staring at his right forearm.

Traynor broke the silence. "You were lucky, son," he said in a low voice. "Next time, stick to the rules."

"Yessir," Tony mumbled.

"That's about all I've got," Traynor said briskly, rising from his chair. He started to turn for the door, then stopped and spoke to P-17 and S-24 again, the businesslike demeanor gone.

"Everyone who knows about your mission is proud as hell of you two. We didn't know if it could be done, but you did it. Because of you, we've learned a lot — and knowledge is the key to beating these things. Well done, Cris. You too, Tony," he said, reaching out to shake each CC's hand in turn. "Now I'll leave you alone so you can go relax for a while."

He opened the door, then turned back to Cris again. "One more thing, P-17. I almost forgot."

"What?"

"The next time you kick one of those things in the teeth . . ."

Cris stiffened. *Now*, when the evaluation was all but over, he was going to get it.

". . . give it a good one for me, will you?"

The Master was surprised initially, but then Its reaction turned to amusement. These humans were persistent, and this time they had actually succeeded in an attack on one of Its outposts. But that meant nothing, since the creature was obviously dysfunctional before the attack.

No, "succeeded" was not the right word. . . .

14

April 25, 2036

The term "R&R," as given in Cris and Tony's itinerary, was a holdover from an earlier, different time when it actually meant something. Conventional soldiers always looked forward to time for "recreation and relaxation," because it meant a few hours or a few days away from the tedium or the danger of their duties.

But Cyborg Commandos didn't need R&R the way human beings did. The standard, periodic sleep period was sufficient to keep their brains in top shape, and their bodies never got fatigued. And, given the situation, CCs could not be allowed to take time off simply for the sake of getting a break. Their routines were repetitious but never dull: a briefing, a mission, a debriefing, possibly a sleep period, then another briefing, and so on.

They were kept almost constantly on the go, because their minds and bodies could take this sort of rigorous activity and because time was crucial. Every minute that a CC spent fighting the invaders was one less minute before the xenoborgs could be exterminated or driven from the planet.

When an R&R slot showed up in a CC's itinerary, it usually meant that he or she was simply supposed to kill some time until that CC's schedule could be dovetailed with some other activity. In this case, Cris assumed that he and Tony were being given an hour of free time because C-12 and O-33 were busy with something else, and all four of them had to be available at the same time for the group briefing session.

"I think I'll go for a stroll," Tony said as he and Cris left the room where their evalutaion had taken place. "Haven't had a chance to see very much of this place yet. Wanna join me?"

"If you don't mind, I'll just go back to quarters, maybe do some reading." He was carefully casual, not wanting Tony to suspect his real feelings. The truth was, Cris wanted some time to think, to try to sort out a few things in his mind, and he thought he couldn't do that and deal with Tony's effervescent chatter at the same time.

"Okay," Tony said cheerfully. "I'll drop by and pick you up just before the briefing."

"Right."

Back in his quarters, Cris made a pretense of

busying himself. He flicked on his videocom screen and called up the latest CCF status report, a compilation of tidbits of information from Cyborg Commando bases around the world. The general tone of the material was the same as ever — CCs almost always killed xenoborgs wherever they were encountered, and once in a while a "unit" was lost in action when it was caught in a crossfire or greatly outnumbered. The forces of Earth had not regained or even penetrated any of the cities occupied by teleborg bases, and had been limited in recent months to fighting — and winning — skirmishes in areas where the xenoborg concentration was relatively light.

He scanned through the reports, looking for the latest news concerning the Manitowoc base, and was upset to discover no mention of his and Tony's mission. He read about other missions that had taken place at roughly the same time, but there was not a word about their incursion into enemy territory and the resultant destruction of the teleborg.

"Why would they keep it a secret?" Cris muttered, searching for a reason. "What have they got against spreading good news?" Individual CCs were never identified in the reports, so Cris wasn't bothered for selfish reasons. He didn't want the credit, but he wanted the rest of the world to know — for its sake — that something had happened that was really worth celebrating.

He thought briefly about contacting the base's communication center and raising a stink, but he figured that wouldn't get him anywhere. If they had a reason for withholding the information, they probably wouldn't tell him what the reason was. And if it was simply a screw-up — although he couldn't imagine how an event of this magnitude could get overlooked — they certainly wouldn't admit that to him, either.

"Oh, what the hell," he said to himself. "Maybe they'll put it online in a little while." He made a mental note to check the Manitowoc report again just before leaving for his briefing, and he tried to convince himself that by then the omission would be corrected.

But he wasn't convinced. It was just one more thing to think about, to be bothered by. And somehow, in a way he couldn't identify, this bit of unsettling information seemed to fit in with the other facts and observations that were troubling him. He lapsed into thought, still staring at the screen but not really seeing what was displayed on it.

First, there was that feeling he had seen behind his mother's eyes when he and Tony returned — a glimmer of something other than joy, which seemed to take the edge off the happiness she was exhibiting outwardly. He knew that Nora's job, her responsibilities, her range of knowledge, far exceeded the scope of his need to know. He didn't expect, or even want, her to tell him every piece of information she was privy to, and maybe the thing that was troubling her — if it was anything at all — had nothing to do with him. But he still couldn't keep from wondering.

Ever since it had occurred to him, he had been trying to discount the fact that his mother had not actually confirmed that the teleborg was killed. Sometimes what people didn't say was more important than what they did say — was this one of those times? Maybe Tony was right; if the aerial assault was as extensive as it had seemed to be, there was no way the thing could have survived, and he should have simply made that assumption the way Tony had. Despite the anxious moments that both he and Tony had experienced, the mission had essentially gone just as planned — so how could it have failed? Still, a small doubt nagged at him.

Then there was Traynor's remark at the end of the evaluation about how "we learned a lot" from the mission. Was that the best he could do? He could have said "we learned how to kill a teleborg" — but he didn't. He made their effort seem more like a fact-finding expedition than the dangerous mission it actually was. Maybe he just didn't express himself fully enough. No, that wasn't like Traynor; the man hardly ever used the wrong words or misspoke. But his little speech at the end had been informal, not a part of the official evaluation, and probably spontaneous. Maybe he wasn't choosing his words carefully, and maybe if he had it to say over again he would be more definite and more specific. . . .

All the "maybes" rolled around in Cris's mind for a few seconds, and then he decided to do something about his insecurity. He bent over the videocom keyboard and tapped out the code that would connect him with the terminal in his mother's office. The response flashed on the screen with unsettling quickness:

UNAVAILABLE UNTIL 1620. QUERY NOTED.

That was not really unusual. Nora Whitaker had a full schedule and couldn't be expected to jump every time someone — even her son — wanted to contact her. Cris considered keying in the query again, and this time tagging it "urgent," but now his uncertainty worked against him in a different way. He couldn't be sure that his question *was* urgent, and "urgent" was not a word that could be used lightly . . . so he didn't use it.

Instead, he typed in a request for Traynor to contact him. As long as he could reach one or the other of them, he could put his mind at ease.

UNAVAILABLE UNTIL 1640.

There was one more thing he could do. This time he asked the comm center to tell him where

Nora Whitaker was. He still had enough time to go to her and ask her in person, so all he needed to know was . . .

UNAVAILABLE UNTIL 1620.

All right, so where is Traynor, then? He touched the keys once more.

UNAVAILABLE UNTIL 1640.

"Oh, terrific," Cris said. "What is this, some kind of a plot?" That was an offhand remark, but it got him thinking again. He couldn't get to either of the people he wanted to talk to, and he would conveniently be in the middle of his mission briefing before they could be reached. He knew it was probably just an unfortunate coincidence. But in his frame of mind he couldn't dismiss the possibility, however slim, that he was deliberately being kept from contacting them, either by their choice or because they were acting on orders from someone else.

He spent the next several minutes trying to talk himself out of being depressed, suspicious, and paranoid.

"Not one of these things is worth worrying about," he said. "I have to keep my imagination under control." But all of "these things" kept running together in his mind; he could no longer think of them individually. They all added up to something — but what?

"Okay," he said, taking another tack. "What's the worst it could be? We didn't kill the teleborg after all, either because we gave it the wrong dosage of food or because we didn't blast it with enough stuff. So we found out how *not* to kill a teleborg, and next time we can learn from our mistakes and do the job right."

"But we didn't *make* any mistakes," the other side of him countered. "It should have worked — it *had* to work. . . ." Cris was so absorbed in arguing with himself that he didn't hear Tony enter the room.

"What's the matter?" said S-24. "Your videocom on the blink?"

Cris whirled and half-rose from his chair before he realized who was talking.

"Hey," Tony said, holding up his hands and taking a step backward. "No need to get hostile."

"Sorry," Cris said. "I was kind of distracted."

"You aren't still being mister gloom-and-doom, are you? I thought you got that out of your system. Heck, I almost blew my own arm off a few hours ago, and you don't see me walking around with my chin on my chest."

"Yeah," Cris acknowledged. "Just how do you get over things so quickly?"

"A simple philosophy. No matter how bad things seem, they're always better than they could be. Try thinking that way and you'll rarely be down — except, of course, when your batteries run out."

"I'll work on it," Cris muttered. Now he regretted not having stayed with Tony during their free hour, because after just a few seconds with his friend he was starting to feel better already.

"Almost time for our next lecture," Tony said. "We better get moving."

"Yeah." Cris got up and started moving toward the door, then checked himself. "Just a minute." He went back to the screen, called up the CCF status report again, and scrolled to the latest news about Manitowoc operatives. Word for word, the screen was the same as the last time he had looked at it.

It was as if his and Tony's mission had never taken place.

15

April 25, 2036

P-17 and S-24 got to the briefing room a few minutes early. As Cris had hoped, John Edwards was already inside.

"Hey, kid!" John called as Cris came through the doorway. "Welcome back!"

"Same to you," Cris said, moving to where C-12 was standing. "You don't look any the worse for wear."

"Nah. It wasn't exactly your standard shoot-'em-up, but they gave the job to the right man, and we got back okay," he said, with a wave of his hand to indicate another CC standing behind him.

"I guess you could say the same about us," Cris said, stepping to one side and motioning for Tony to come forward. "John, this is Corporal S-24, also known as my good friend Tony Minelli in his previous incarnation. Tony, this is Lieutenant C-12 — the man you've heard so much about."

"All of it impressive if not astounding, I'm sure," John said, offering his hand as Tony started to salute. "You can dispense with that," the lieutenant continued. "After all, we're not exactly regular army, are we?"

"No, sir, I guess not," said Tony, grasping John's hand briefly.

"And this," John announced, "is my new friend Sergeant O-33 — the woman you've heard absolutely nothing about."

Cris had noticed something vaguely different about the other CC, but it didn't click until John introduced her. O-33's body was virtually identical to his own, although slightly smaller in proportion. The face was a bit thinner and more delicate, the hair a couple of inches longer. There was no practical reason why CCs of different genders should have different appearances, and from a distance one looked the same as another. But it did help, in close contact, to know at a glance whether the cybernetic soldier you were talking to was male or female.

"Hello, gentlemen," she said, extending her hand first to Cris and then to Tony. Her eyes met P-17's again and she added, "The lieutenant has told me quite a bit about you, and I must say I am impressed." Her voice was stiff and mechanical, not human-sounding. Cris supposed that either her voice simulator was in need of repair or that she had never been equipped with one. Whatever the reason, he hoped she would be given a real voice during the refitting session scheduled to follow the briefing. O-33 looked something like a woman, but right now she sounded too much like a robot to suit him.

"Errr . . . thank you, sergeant," Cris said, his uneasiness evident in his hesitant response.

"Please don't be put off by the way I sound," said O-33. Pointing to her throat, she added, "I've been having trouble with it off and on for the last few weeks. I understand they're finally going to install a brand-new voicebox during the refit. And while they're at it, they're going to fix my normal-range auditory circuits. If it's any consolation, you sound pretty much the same to me as I do to you right now."

"I'm sorry," Cris said, "but I'm glad to know everything will be okay later. And," he added with a sidelong glance at John, "I'm happy to find out that the good lieutenant speaks more highly of me when I'm not around than he does when I'm in his presence."

"Aw, it wasn't quite like that, kid," John said. "I was actually giving her a short version of my illustrious cybernetic career, and your name came up a few times."

"Yeah? Like the time I hauled your metallic butt off that grenade-infested rooftop? Like the time I—"

C-12 and O-33 looked toward the doorway. Cris stopped in mid-sentence and turned his head. Into the room walked General Garrison carrying a slim folder, with Nora Whitaker on his heels and Traynor right behind her.

"What the . . ." Cris said under his breath. Traynor and his mother were not "unavailable" — they were right here, right now!

"Sit down," the general ordered briskly. "We have a lot to do." He moved to a chair behind the table at the front of the room, Nora and Traynor sat off to the side, and the four CCs faced the general in oversized chairs designed for their larger-than-human bodies.

The general cleared his throat. "I have a statement to read, after which I will entertain any reasonable questions, and then we will proceed to the subject of your next mission." He opened the folder and began to read. Cris listened, his mind racing as he absorbed the man's words.

"Several hours ago, at the conclusion of the infiltration mission undertaken by P-17 and S-24, conventional military forces of the Trans-American Union were able to stage a successful aerial raid on a teleborg base located on the northern edge of the Milwaukee urban area."

Successful . . . then the teleborg *was* killed! Finally, what he had been waiting to hear!

"Nearly eighty percent of the projectiles targeted against the creature struck it, or struck close enough to do some incidental damage. Losses in personnel and reusable equipment amounted to less than five percent, making the mission an unqualified success from that standpoint."

From *that* standpoint? It was great to hear that not too many men died and very few planes were lost, but what did he mean by those last three words?

"The teleborg sustained massive damage. Most of its technological armament and defense systems were destroyed or rendered useless, and low-altitude reconnaissance photographs indicate that its body was torn and ruptured in dozens of places. We have every reason to believe that if the attack had not been interrupted, the creature would have been dead in a matter of minutes."

Would have?! Now what was the man trying to say? Cris fought to keep himself under control, and he saw Tony shift slightly in his seat as though he was trying to do the same.

"Unfortunately, the teleborg evacuated seven minutes after the assault began. It lifted off and flew for several dozen miles due south at an altitude of no more than five hundred feet, traveling too low and too fast for the rest of the assault force to make course adjustments in time to try to shoot it out of the sky. Our fighters almost caught up with it — they had it on visual and were about to open fire — when the thing shot straight up. It was out of the atmosphere about three minutes later. Long-range tracking indicates that it is currently some twenty thousand miles away from the planet, coasting on a trajectory that will cause it to intercept or impact with the moon."

Cris was crushed, too despondent to say or do anything at the moment. What good did it do to blast the hell out of the thing if it could simply pull up its roots any time it wanted and cruise up and out of danger? Now he had a pretty clear picture of what had actually happened, and he could put some of the puzzle together, but there were still some things he needed to know.

"It is our judgment that this was not a singular tactic, but rather one that could, and would, be employed by any teleborg that is made the target of a similar assault. Part of the objective was realized, in the sense that the alien was driven off the surface of the planet. But we must assume that unless the teleborgs are conclusively killed, they will use some means to heal and repair themselves and eventually return.

"That, in brief, is the state of affairs. Questions — one at a time, please."

"How could it get away?" asked John in a clinical tone. Sure, he's not upset, Cris thought sourly. He can afford to be cool and detached — because he's not the one whose mission got screwed up!

"The strategy of dropping the nutrients must have worked," the general said, "because if the thing had not been sluggish and disoriented, our projectiles could not have gotten through its defenses. According to the biologists, its escape was a form of survival instinct — a drive that's even stronger than its appetite. In other words, it would rather stay alive than keep eating. And the underside of its body, where its fuel tanks and propulsion gear are located, was still relatively intact after the first few minutes of the assault. So, when it sensed that remaining stationary any longer was going to lead to its death, the thing just took off."

"So why didn't you just hit it with bigger bombs to start with?" Tony asked, recrimination dripping from the words.

"First of all," the general said icily, "we don't have that many 'big bombs' right now. Ninety percent of the world's conventional military equipment, including munitions, was destroyed when these . . . things . . . invaded, and it has taken a lot of time and a lot of lives to build back to the level we're at now. Second of all, we don't use 'big bombs' for the same reason we don't use nuclear weapons or biological warfare." The general paused and took a deep breath, as though trying to keep his temper under control. He was frowning, and spoke in a louder voice, when he resumed talking.

"There were people living, trying to hold on, within a couple of miles of that creature — people who could have been hurt or killed by the concussion from a massive explosion. There's not much point in killing these things if we have to wipe out the rest of the human race and devastate the planet in the process." General Garrison was nearly livid by the time he finished, and Corporal S-24 was thoroughly intimidated. Cris thought he saw Tony visibly shrink in his seat as the general ground out his last sentence. Then he realized the man was done, and he jumped in, ever so politely, with the question that was uppermost in his mind.

"Why are they here?" he asked, cocking his head toward where his mother and Traynor sat.

"Let me answer that," Nora said, rising quickly to her feet. The general frowned slightly, then motioned for her to go ahead.

"I knew the truth when I saw you this morning," she said, looking directly at her son. "But I was under orders not to tell you." Here she glanced toward the general, as if indicating where the blame for her deception should be placed.

"I don't know if I could have told you anyway," she continued, her voice quivering slightly. "You were so happy . . . you didn't deserve to have your moment of triumph ruined — not by me or by anyone else."

"Aw, mom . . ." Cris started to say something consoling, but Traynor's voice cut in.

"They had to tell me what happened," the man said, "because I would be talking to both of you about the mission. They didn't want me to lie to you unknowingly, so they filled me in. But they didn't want me to tell you the whole truth, either."

"So you said 'we learned a lot.' How comforting," Cris said sullenly.

"That was true, but it was a mistake," Traynor admitted. "I shouldn't have said anything at all, and I'm sorry I opened my mouth."

Cris could tell Traynor was sincere, and that made him regret his last remark. He was about to return the "I'm sorry" when the general harrumphed and again took control.

"The answer to the question is simply this," he said, gesturing to Nora to take her seat. "Both of them have important roles in the mission you are about to undertake, so they are just as entitled as you to have any information concerning that mission. And I hate to repeat myself, so we're all going through this at the same time. Any other *reasonable* questions?" he concluded, looking at P-17 and then S-24 as he raised one eyebrow.

Tony kept quiet, but Cris wasn't done — and, reasonable or not, he wanted to pursue the subject that his mother and Traynor had brought up. "Why all the secrecy?" he asked. "Why couldn't you just tell us straight out that we failed?"

"You didn't fail," the general said firmly. "You did what you were supposed to do. It's not your fault — or anybody else's fault — that the last phase of the plan didn't work as well as the first. As for the secrecy: It is absolutely crucial to the success of your upcoming mission that the truth about this matter be known by as few individuals as possible.

If someone had revealed the facts to you without authorization and outside the confines of this meeting, you might have let it slip to someone else, and that might have started an uncontrollable chain reaction.

"We could not let you know the truth until we could, at the same time, impress upon you the need to keep it to yourselves. I know you've heard this sort of speech before" — Cris chuckled wryly inside, remembering the general's words about how he hated to repeat himself — "but this is different. You could talk about anything you've ever done, you could shout it from the rooftops, and it wouldn't be as damaging to our cause as a single, whispered sentence concerning any of what you learn in this room today."

"But why—"

"I think any further questions you may have on the topic will be addressed in the next part of this briefing, lieutenant. Let's restrict ourselves to the substance of my earlier statement, please."

"Okay," said John. "What kind of motive power do these things use?"

"Our best guess is a combination — two propulsion systems for two different purposes. The thing was going no faster than a jet aircraft when it was near the ground — we know that because we were able to keep pace with it after it got the head start. Then it slowed to a crawl for a few seconds, and some other system kicked in that sent it straight up. The fighter pilots in the vicinity detected intense heat coming out of huge nozzles in the creature's underside — some sort of super-powerful, super-efficient rocket engines. The pilots sent missiles up after it, but the damn thing outran them like they were stones from a slingshot."

"Do they have any weak spots?" That from John again. Cris couldn't understand why he kept wanting to know more about teleborgs. What good would the knowledge be if they didn't have a way of getting them to hold still long enough to blast them to bits? Still, the general had been answering John's questions completely and with uncharacteristic civility. Maybe C-12 was on to something. . . .

The general smiled thinly. "If I had to guess, I'd say their strength and their weakness are one and the same. If we could get one or two clean shots at the underside of one of them, its fuel tanks would go up like a blast furnace filled with dynamite."

"But we can't do that when it's on the ground," Tony pointed out.

The smile on the general's face grew a bit wider. "That's exactly right, son. And that, if there are no further questions, brings me directly to the heart of the matter. . . ."

* * *

For the next several minutes, General Garrison had the floor to himself. No one else said a word while he went through a step-by-step, fairly detailed description of what the mission involved and how the four CCs and two human beings would interact to accomplish their objective.

The general spoke in a carefully maintained monotone; the military jargon he used to convey the orders was usually dry and occasionally wordy and overblown, as information of this sort tended to be. But none of that kept Cris from feeling chills inside as he listened and comprehended the full importance and difficulty of what they were being sent out to do. He imagined that the others in the room, humans and cyborgs alike, felt the same way — how could they *not* be hopeful, anxious, and more than a little scared about what lay before them?

The general straightened in his chair and lifted his eyes from the folder in front of him. Here comes the big finish, Cris thought. The pep talk, I hope. I could use one right now. . . .

"You four will head west shortly after the conclusion of your next sleep period," the general said to the cybernetic soldiers in front of him. "You won't see any of us, any of this"— he waved his arm to indicate the whole of the base —"again for quite some time. Except for scheduled communications, you will be out of touch with this headquarters for a longer period of time than any Cyborg Commandos have ever existed in the field before. And, of course, you will have access to no resources other than what you carry with you when you leave . . ."

Cris had to suppress a chuckle at the general's use of the phrase "in the field." Now there's a piece of jargon · that's about to become outdated, he thought. But I don't suppose that will stop them from using it.

". . . and what you may be able to scavenge along the way. By the way, we have no reason to think that this extended stay away from the base will prevent you from seeing the mission through or hinder you in any way. If it wasn't possible for you to stay out for two to four weeks, we wouldn't consider attempting it. All of you are too valuable to risk losing for that reason. Being killed in action is a chance each of you takes every time you go outside — but we aren't about to let you simply run out of power and expire in the middle of a wasteland somewhere in North Dakota."

Sensing that the general was at the end of a complete thought, John raised a hand to get his attention and then, without waiting for acknowledgment, spoke up. "Why us?" he asked.

Good for you, Cris thought. Maybe that will steer the old goat into saying something uplifting.

"Because you are the four most qualified . . . people . . . this base has at its disposal right now," the general said to John. Then he continued as if he was talking to someone else, and the four of them were not in the room. "C-12 and P-17 have drawn the assignment on the basis of general merit; they are the best two examples we've ever seen at this base of what a Cyborg Commando can do when the technology is utilized with the utmost in skill, efficiency, and good judgment. O-33, although only a recent addition to the Manitowoc corps, is the most experienced unit we have in the area of field repair. S-24 is on the team because the mission requires an S-type unit, and we don't have any others in . . . in one piece right now." John and O-33 exchanged a brief glance; her former partner must have been the only other operational S-unit assigned to the base.

"Excuse me, sir." Now that John had broken the ice, Cris figured it was okay for him to say something, too. "I appreciate the compliment, but I wonder about your use of the word 'drawn.' The last time John . . . the last time C-12 and I received orders for unusual and dangerous missions, we were given a chance to decline. This time it seems as though we don't have any choice."

"Indeed," said the general. "Before, you were the best candidates for the jobs we gave you, but others could have undertaken those missions if you had turned them down. This time there's too much riding on the outcome for us to give you the option of backing out. In addition to being responsible for millions of dollars worth of virtually irreplaceable equipment, you four are also the custodians of the future of the human race. If we don't send up the four best soldiers we've got, the mission will in all probability not succeed. And the mission must succeed. Therefore, as you put it, you have no choice."

"Thank you, sir," Cris said respectfully, with the slightest tinge of sarcasm.

"Don't thank me," the general shot back. "Thank those bastard aliens." He stood up and strode quickly out of the room.

With a few minutes to spare before their refit was scheduled, the four CCs did not need to leave that quickly. They rose slowly as Nora and Traynor walked over to meet them. The man was the first to speak.

"We'll do as much as we can for you from back here," he said. "But the general is basically right. Once you leave here, you're on your own. Do you think you can do it?"

"Hell, yes," John spat. "You're looking at the cream of the cybernetic crop, remember? The more we succeed, the more they expect us to succeed. It's a vicious circle, which if they have their way won't end until we're sitting on top of a high-tech scrap heap."

"Come on, John," Cris said. "We've been through a lot and we're still here. We can handle this, too."

"You're right, kid. We have been through a lot — too much to suit me. Don't forget, I've been looking at the world through artificial eyes four times longer than you have. Well, I came to a carefully considered decision during the general's monologue, somewhere between the words 'liftoff' and 'splashdown.' This is it for me. When we get back — and you'll notice I *did* say 'when' — I'm going under the knife. I'm gonna get my brain put back where it belongs, even if all they do is plant me in the ground when the operation's over."

"No!" said Nora plaintively. "Don't think that way, John."

"You have to understand," he said, taking her by the arm and steering her to another part of the room. Cris followed them, leaving the other three members of the group to talk among themselves.

"I need to be myself again," C-12 continued in a more gentle tone, putting a finger to Nora's lips to prevent her from interrupting. "I need to know how it feels to hold you with *real* hands, to kiss you with—" He broke off, realizing that Cris was standing a couple of paces away.

"Don't stop on my account, John," Cris said warmly. "I'm not exactly ignorant of what's been going on for the last year or so. I know how you feel about my mother, and I think I can understand why—"

"But you can't take that chance, John," Nora cut in. "The process is far from perfected, and you might . . . I'd rather have you the way you are for right now than not at all."

"I do understand that," John said. "But you don't know what it's like from this side."

212

"Do you think you're the only one who's frustrated?" she said, her tone becoming harsh. "Believe me, it's no fun having *both* of the men you love locked up inside artificial bodies. I want you back, too, but you have to wait. As soon as we know for sure how to reverse the transplant, I will personally demand that you and Cris be the first—"

"Excuse me, sir." O-33's metallic voice rang out as she tapped P-17 on the shoulder. "I didn't want to interrupt, but we really should be getting on to that refit."

"You're right, sergeant," said John. "We'll talk some more about this when we get back," he added to Nora. Then he headed for the door without waiting for a reply.

Cris and Tony said quick goodbyes to Nora and Traynor and made arrangements to get together once more before they left the base. Then the other three CCs left the room together and walked down the corridor toward the refit station, Cris and O-33 side by side with Tony bringing up the rear.

"Believe it or not," O-33 said to Cris, "I'm looking forward to this mission."

"Yeah, I guess I am too."

"I wish Lieutenant C-12 felt the same way."

"Oh, don't worry about John. When the shooting starts, there's nobody I'd rather have on my side. And you *can* call him John, you know, even though he's an officer. By the way, what's your—"

"If you don't mind, sir," said O-33, "I'd rather

stick to designations instead of names; just consider it a quirk of mine. In fact, I wish I didn't know C-12's name, I wish you hadn't introduced the corporal as 'Tony,' and I wish I hadn't overheard your mother refer to you as Rick."

"Huh?"

"Isn't that your name? I thought that's what I heard her say. Must be these maladjusted ears of mine," she said, tapping her temple with the heel of her hand to cover her embarrassment.

"No, it's Cris. Cris Holman."

O-33 took one more step, then froze in her tracks. Cris was three paces ahead of her before he realized she wasn't beside him any more. As he whirled and looked back, S-24 was already examining her to see if she had suffered some sort of massive power failure.

"What happened?" Cris asked.

"Well, it looks to me," Tony said, "as if the lady has fainted."

16

April 25-26, 2036

A few seconds after O-33's organic brain lost consciousness, her internal computer took over and began to put one mechanical foot in front of the other.

"Oh, good," Tony said, falling into step behind her once more. "At least we won't have to carry her."

"What do you mean 'we,' skinny?" Cris called back over his shoulder.

"Hey, man, I may be thin, but—"

"Uh-oh," Cris interrupted. "We'd better get some help." He was trying to ease O-33 around a corner to get her headed for the refit station, but her internal computer was insisting on continuing straight ahead. He wasn't sure what would happen if he tried to force the body to make the right-angle turn, so the safest course was to let technicians handle the problem.

Leaving O-33 to plod mechanically through the corridor, Cris and Tony headed at a fast walk for the refit station, which was only a short distance away. They weren't worried about her because they knew her internal computer wouldn't let her do anything dangerous or dumb, such as tumbling down a stairway or walking into a wall. As long as she didn't get into a life-threatening situation — which was virtually impossible inside the complex — she would continue to wander more or less randomly until her brain regained consciousness naturally or until technicians could intercept her and get her systems working properly again.

When they got to the refit station, Cris explained what had happened, and a couple of men in white lab coats gathered up a few pieces of equipment and hurried out the door.

"What did you do to her?" Tony asked his friend as they waited for their examinations to begin.

"Nothing. We were walking along, making small talk about names and designations, and she just blipped out."

"Well, she seems to have a few little things wrong with her," Tony said, referring to the obvious ways in which O-33 was in need of repair. "I hope this isn't something we'll have to worry about or something that will affect the mission."

"Don't sweat it," Cris said, even though he didn't

really believe his own words. "These guys can fix anything — right, guys?"

"We do our best," said one of the technicians as he came up and motioned Cris over to a panel laden with sockets and switches. John was in a similar-looking location on the other side of the room, already being probed and scrutinized, and Tony was being led toward another area several feet away from Cris. "Time to get things moving."

Even if a Cyborg Commando didn't appear to be damaged or defective, he or she had to go through a session like this every ten to fifteen days — or, as in this case, immediately prior to setting out on a mission that was unusually dangerous or required an extended stay away from the base. "Refit" was something of a misnomer, since the procedure was really only a thorough examination to find out if all the mechanical and electronic parts of a CC were in top working order. But the technicians who worked in the refit station were obsessively meticulous — they prided themselves on always finding at least one small thing that needed adjustment, repair, or replacement.

Obviously, Cris thought as he stood silent and motionless while the testers did their jobs, these guys have never heard of the old adage "If it ain't broke, don't fix it." But he appreciated their devotion to duty and their attention to detail, and he never complained about getting a refit even when he felt fine — as he did now.

"I have a question," Cris said in a low voice. The technicians didn't appreciate being engaged in conversation when they were concentrating, but it wasn't strictly forbidden.

"Yeah," replied the man who was examining him, looking up from his work briefly.

"If you guys are so good, how can someone like O-33 have so many things wrong with her?"

"Humidity and salt," the man said with a bit of exasperation. "Two things we didn't have to worry about until they brought in the transfers from Texas. They're from Corpus Christi — right on the gulf."

"So?"

"So when they get damaged and that wet, salty air gets inside their systems, it clogs things up, corrodes the contacts. Sometimes a good cleaning takes care of the problem, but sometimes it crops up again and we end up having to put in new parts. That girl's in worse shape than most because, from what they tell me, she likes to open herself up and do her own repairs. Every time she did that down south, she got even more moisture and salt in her systems."

"Is she going to be okay?" Cris was concerned about O-33's condition for her own sake, but more than that he wanted reassurance that she wouldn't suffer some sort of breakdown and endanger their mission.

"Nothing to worry about," the man said with a

thin smile, sensing the main reason behind the question. "By the time she leaves here, she'll be in top working order. Now let me get back to work."

*　*　*

The four members of the mission team were housed in special quarters for the sleep periods that would precede their egress from the base. This was necessary, as they had been informed during their briefing, because while their brains slept they would undergo one more bit of preventive maintenance — something that couldn't be done while the brain was conscious.

In a process analogous to the simultaneous draining and refilling of a reservoir, but much more sophisticated and complicated, each CC's supply of life-support and auxiliary chemicals was reconditioned and replenished. The synthetic blood that kept their brains alive was pumped out and circulated through a filtering and cleaning system. The vitamins, nutrient supplements, and other chemicals stored in each unit's internal pharmacy were tested and, if necessary, augmented or replaced.

Every precaution was being taken to ensure that when this mission began, each Cyborg Commando involved would be in the same perfect condition that he or she had been just after going through the transplant operation — brand-new, or better, if that was possible. Although CCs were kept in good working order as a matter of standard procedure, rarely were they put through maintenance programs of this intensity and scope. The approach and methodology of the doctors and technicians were reminiscent of the way human beings had been tested and conditioned nearly seventy years ago, in the early days of the manned space program — and that was an appropriate parallel indeed, because, if all went well, these four Cyborg Commandos would be among the first of their kind to journey into the void beyond the atmosphere of Earth.

* * *

When P-17 awoke, he had no trouble coming fully alert in a matter of seconds. Not only was he ready to go physically and psychologically, he was absolutely brimming with eagerness and enthusiasm. He knew this was because the doctors had purposely fed his brain a small dose of an antidepressant drug — something that wasn't normally necessary and probably wasn't essential now. But instead of dwelling on the fact that his extremely good mood was at least in part artificially induced, Cris Holman submerged that knowledge deep within his consciousness and chose to savor the feeling for everything it was worth.

When he reached the debarkation area, Tony and Traynor were already there. "Good *morning*, lieutenant!" S-24 shouted. "Isn't it a beautiful day for a cruise in the country?"

"I'm sure it is," said Cris wryly, "despite the fact that it's only a little after midnight."

"Hah!" Tony scoffed. "You can try, but there's no way you're going to burst my bubble."

"I don't think there's a force on Earth that could do that," Cris said. Then he addressed Traynor. "Are you sure he didn't get too big a shot of joy juice?"

"I'm sure it was no more than he needed," said the man.

"Well, I'd get a second opinion on that if I were you," Cris replied. Just then John and Nora walked in the room through different doors.

"Hail, hail, the gang's all here — except for the lovely O-33," Tony chirped. Then he lifted his arm as if checking an imaginary wristwatch and added playfully in Nora's direction, "Isn't it just like a woman to be late?"

"She has her reasons, S-24," Nora said with feigned reproach.

The five of them spent the next few minutes exchanging small talk and wishes for luck and success. Optimism and good cheer were the order of the day. Cris was happy to note that his mother seemed to exhibit none of the anxiety she usually felt before seeing him off on a mission — so much the better because he knew her good mood was not chemically assisted the way his was.

And C-12 had apparently shaken off the troubles that had caused him to make the pronouncement he had made in the briefing room. He was cocky and full of quips — the same old John. When Cris made a remark to that effect, John was quick to set the record straight.

"It's not the drugs talking, kid," he said. "I decided something before I went to sleep, and that was this: There's no sense in worrying about later until later gets here. Right now we have a job to do, and we mechanical marvels are not going to think about anything else until that job is done. Right?"

"Right!" echoed Cris and Tony in unison.

"I agree," said a soft, feminine voice from across the room.

Cris turned toward the sound. If he had a heart, it would have skipped a beat.

Standing just inside the doorway was a female Cyborg Commando who could only be O-33; no one else would have been allowed entry. But this was not the same CC he had last seen shuffling mechanically down the hallway. Except for the torso, where her brain capsule was located, she looked like she had been given all-new parts — which was why her refit took slightly longer than normal. Her arms, legs, and head were in pristine condition, showing none of the normal, harmless wear and tear of a body that had been used for some time. Cris's impression as he first laid eyes

222

on her was that she had just stepped off an assembly line — which wasn't far from the truth.

But even before he had seen her, he had heard her — and that had left an impression he couldn't deal with. Even as his logical mind told him it was impossible, his emotional mind insisted that he *knew* that voice. . . .

Fighting to maintain his self-control, he stared at O-33 and said evenly, "Say something else."

She hesitated, and her voice broke as she started to speak. "I never . . . I never thought I'd see you again, Cris."

By the time she said his name, Cris was rushing toward her. While everyone else in the room looked on in bewildered amazement, P-17 reflexively threw his arms around O-33 and was crying with uncontrolled joy. "Oh, God, Maura. You're alive!"

17

April 26, 2036

Even though he had made the promise just seconds earlier, Cris had forgotten about his vow to think about nothing but the mission ahead of him. All he cared about now was that the woman he had loved — the woman he still did love — was in his arms again.

"This is a miracle," he whispered. "I can't believe it."

O-33 stepped back from his embrace, raised her arms, and cradled his chin in her hands. The gesture sent a quiet thrill through Cris, just as it always had in days gone by. "I couldn't believe it at first either," she said. "But it's real."

All Cris could manage in reply was a soft moan of pleasure.

Maura brought her hands down from his face to

his shoulders, gripping them gently as she looked up into his eyes. "Now, don't you go swooning the way I did. Holding you is one thing, but I don't want to have to carry you out the door when we leave."

Her gaze shifted to a point slightly behind him, and Cris suddenly remembered they were not alone in the room. He turned his head slightly to acknowledge John, who was standing just behind his left shoulder with Nora at his side. "I think we all have a pretty good idea what's going on here," C-12 said. "But would you like to fill us in anyway?"

A flush of embarrassment swept through Cris's mind, but it was gone by the time he had turned around and positioned himself at O-33's side, wrapping his left arm around her shoulders. "You've all heard me talk about Maura," he told the group. "Well . . . here she is!"

Nora was the first to respond. "I'm so happy for you, Cris," she said, stepping forward and touching his forearm tenderly. Then she held out a hand to Maura, apparently feeling that a reintroduction was necessary. "Hello. I'm Cris's mother. Please call me Nora."

"Yes," said O-33 hesitantly. "But . . ."

"My *real* mother," Cris told her. "It's a little confusing, but I'll tell you about it later."

John and Tony stepped forward to greet Maura, and then Traynor did the same. The man seemed outwardly as cordial and as happy as the others were, but Cris detected a tinge of concern in his expression at the same time. After expressing his congratulations to Cris and then Maura individually, he addressed both of them.

"I have to ask something," he said, "and I need honest answers. Do you two think you can go on this mission together and keep your wits about you?"

Reality hit Cris between the eyes, and he responded instinctively. "Oh, no," he said, looking at Maura. "You have to stay. You have to be safe—"

Maura raised a finger to his lips, cutting him off. "Wait, Cris. Give yourself a minute to think about it. I felt that way right after I found out who you were — after they tracked me down and woke me up, that is. Now that I had you back, I didn't want you to go out and risk your life on this mission."

"But I *have* to go—"

"We *both* have to go," Maura said. "That's the point. And even if one of us could get out of it, what difference would it make? Look at us, Cris. We're committed. We can't take ourselves off active duty and expect the people who run this place to let us stay in our quarters just because we want each other to be safe — and every time we go outside, whether on this mission or some other one, we're risking our lives. I think we have to make the best of this situation, and the best arrangement I can think of is for the two of us to be together in the field. That way we can help each other."

"Well, what about you?" Traynor turned his attention to Cris.

Cris took a few seconds to think before answering. Then he turned to Traynor. "In different ways and for different reasons, I love everyone in this room — yes, even you, doc. Those feelings have never kept me from doing a good job before, and they won't hinder me now.

"Now I have one more person to love than I did a little while ago, and I could look at that as meaning that I have that much more to lose if I fail — but I'd rather see it as having more to gain by succeeding. Besides, if fate has thrown us together on this escapade, who am I to say that we shouldn't stay together?"

Traynor studied P-17's face for a few seconds, as if searching for a clue that Cris wasn't being honest with himself. He can't read my expression, Cris thought, so what *is* he looking for?

Finally the man spoke. "Is that all you have to say?"

"Well, I could make a five-minute speech," Cris responded, "but I think that sums it up."

"You're sure?"

"I'm sure."

"Then so am I," Traynor said, his face breaking into a warm smile. "Now, what do you say we get this show on the road?"

After one more round of goodbyes and wishes for success, the four CCs entered the accessway, climbed aboard the vehicle waiting for them, and headed for the surface.

* * *

Phase one of the mission would be the most unexciting part — or, at least, everyone hoped it would be uneventful. Before the members of the team could put the big plan into effect, they first had to travel a little more than six hundred miles — from Manitowoc, on the shore of Lake Michigan in east central Wisconsin, to a desolate spot in the wilderness of eastern North Dakota.

To maintain the secrecy that the mission required, they had to cover the distance as inconspicuously as possible; a quartet of Cyborg Commandos openly ambling along on a cross-country trek would certainly attract surveillance by xenoborgs, if not an outright attack. So, they had been provided with a very ordinary-looking means of conveyance — a medium-sized civilian truck with a small compartment for the driver and one passenger plus a spacious cargo bed.

The driver's seat had been stripped down to its frame, and the upper part of S-24's body was fastened to the metal supports by a pair of quick-release clamps. The controls had been modified so they could all be hand-operated. All of this was necessary because the driver's compartment was sized for a human being, and the overly large legs of a Cyborg Commando would never fit into the space available.

"Settle back, y'all," Tony called as he threw the switch that sent current into the battery-powered engine. "Here we go!" S-24's thin torso was covered by a shabby jacket, and he wore a short wig and a battered hat atop his head. From even a short distance, he would appear to be an unimposing farmer or merchant, coaxing his old truck along on some inconsequential errand. Behind him in the cargo area, concealed by a canvas cover that could be pulled back at a second's notice, were the other three CCs and the rest of S-24's body.

The truck also carried an assortment of equipment and supplies, consisting mostly of spare parts, in case their bodies became damaged or disabled, plus a large bank of solar batteries that would provide electrical power for the truck and the cyborgs themselves, in the event that they found it necessary to recharge along the way.

They had been allotted between three and four days to make the journey, which would have been an easy schedule to keep in normal circumstances. But they were operating under restrictions and handicaps that made it likely they'd need most, if not all, of that time to get where they were going.

First, they had to stay off major highways, because those were the routes patrolled most often by scavenging xenoborgs. Sticking to back roads would increase the distance of the trip substantially, and there was always the chance that they'd have to backtrack or go out of their way to get around places where the roads had been torn up or blocked.

Second, they had been ordered to travel no faster than forty miles per hour except in a life-threatening situation. Again, this was to avoid attracting undue attention — they didn't want to appear as though they were in a great hurry to get where they were going.

And third, they had to operate the truck only at night unless they got far behind schedule and were forced to make up for lost time. They were less likely to be accosted by xenoborgs in the darkness, since most of the creatures did not have infrared sensors or other kinds of detection equipment, and the creatures were habitually more active in the heat of the day than at night. During the daytimes, they were supposed to find an inconspicuous place to park the truck and sequester themselves a short distance away, making the vehicle look as though it had been abandoned. Xenoborgs generally did not approach vehicles or locations where no human beings could be heard or seen, so the truck would be fairly safe even when they weren't inside it. If any creatures did approach with the seeming intent of damaging it or its contents, then the CCs would be forced to open fire and try to kill or drive away the marauders. But again, this was not a desirable course of action, since then the xeno-borgs might come to realize that the truck was much more important than it appeared to be.

Tony's initial exuberance dissipated quickly once they got under way. He discovered that no matter which road he selected, their route was strewn with cracks and potholes — highway maintenance had not exactly been a high priority for the last year or so. Every time the truck hit a large obstruction, the vehicle bounced and shuddered as though it was about to fall apart — and S-24 spat out a curse or a complaint under his breath.

"Jeez!" he hissed after the truck lurched over one particularly wide crevice in a narrow concrete roadway. "Is this the best they could do for us?" he continued, not expecting to be overheard. "If this rattletrap makes it through six hundred miles, I'll be a—"

"This 'rattletrap' is in very good shape," said John from the back of the truck. It was similar to vehicles that C-12 had used a couple of times before — equipped with steel-reinforced, puncture-proof tires; each pair of wheels supported by double axles of tempered steel that could withstand a dynamite blast without bending or twisting; an armor-plated undercarriage that could take a direct hit from a boulder without causing any harm to the mechanical and electronic parts that the shielding covered. "It's only *supposed* to look and sound like it's falling apart."

"Well," said Tony, still disgruntled, "you could have fooled me."

"Not exactly a difficult thing to do, corporal," John shot back with friendly sarcasm. "Now, would you keep your complaints to yourself and concentrate on going *around* some of these bumps instead of *over* them? We're being tossed around like popcorn back here."

Tony muttered something unintelligible and dropped the subject while Cris and Maura shared a chuckle over the exchange that had just taken place. "Do these two always talk to each other like that?" she asked between giggles.

"Believe it or not," Cris said, "they haven't known each other very long — but I'd say they're getting along remarkably well in spite of that."

"The kid does have spunk," John observed in a low voice. "And don't tell him this, but I think they could have made this rattletrap a little more easy to ride in."

"Thank you, sir!" Tony called back with exaggerated sincerity.

"Why, you little eavesdropper—"

"Please, sir. I'm trying to concentrate."

* * *

Except for the interludes where John or Tony had something to say, Cris and Maura spent their first couple of hours in the back of the truck bringing each other up to date on what had happened to them in the last fifteen months. As he talked and listened, Cris's emotions swung from one extreme to the other and back again, his joy and relief at finding Maura a sharp contrast to the sadness and horror that came over him when he recalled, verbally and in his mind's eye, the terrible sights and sounds he had witnessed when the invaders had first descended.

The world had turned inside out on January 13, 2035, when transports carrying xenoborgs first appeared in the sky above the Earth. Cris and Maura had been students at the University of Wisconsin campus at Whitewater, and had fallen in love shortly after meeting the previous September. On that fateful Saturday, Cris had left Maura alone at her apartment and headed for his family's home in Delavan, about twenty miles away. He was looking forward to a family dinner in celebration of his little sister Sara's birthday. But when he got to the house, he found it in the process of being overrun by a small group of the alien monsters.

He looked on, virtually helpless, while first his father and then his stepmother were grabbed and killed by the creatures. Then with his sister hidden in the basement, he used himself as bait to lure the monsters away from the house. He circled back and managed to escape with Sara in his father's truck. By the time he got to Whitewater, hoping to find and rescue Maura, that city had been set upon by other xenoborgs, and the residential area where Maura lived was in a shambles.

"I looked for you," he said. "But all I could find was . . ." He paused, unable to continue.

"What, Cris?"

"I found the ankle bracelet I gave you. There was . . . it was still around part of a leg!" he blurted out. "How could—"

"Oh, no," Maura said softly and sympathetically. "That was . . . that was Barbara," she added, referring to a mutual friend who lived in Maura's apartment building. "She dropped in, and I invited her to spend the night. She saw the bracelet and insisted on trying it on. Then there was a big commotion outside, and the building started to come down around us. We ran to get out, and we got separated. That was the last I ever saw of her. . . ." Now it was Maura's turn to pause and gather herself. When Cris sensed that she could go on, he prompted her with a question.

"Where did you go?"

"I went looking for you," she said. "All the phones were dead, so I stole a car — I figured it didn't make any difference — and headed for your house."

"Oh, no," Cris said, piecing together some of the puzzle in his mind. "You mean—"

"At just about the time you were trying to find me in Whitewater, I was getting to your house. I hoped you'd be safe there, but when I saw your car by the side of the road a couple of miles away from the house I got a very bad feeling. Then, when I saw what was left of . . . I didn't see how anyone could have survived."

After that, Maura headed south, because the sketchy news reports she had picked up on the car radio indicated that the invaders were less numerous in that part of the country. The car broke down in southern Illinois, and for the next two days she continued to make her way southward by hitching rides.

Finally, in central Louisiana, she came upon an army transport headed for Corpus Christi, Texas, and she learned from the men and women in the truck about an underground complex in that city where "super-soldiers" were being created by placing human brains inside powerful and sophisticated electromechanical bodies.

"I knew a little bit about these cyborgs," she said. "Enough to make me decide that volunteering for the program was the most sensible thing I could do. I had no family, wouldn't have been able to find my friends ever again, and I was sure I had lost you. Basically, I decided to join the battle against the xenoborgs because there was nothing left for me to live for, and I figured I'd rather go down fighting than starve to death or get killed before I could take any of them with me."

"That doesn't sound like you," Cris said. "It's such a cold attitude."

"Oh, it *was* cold. That's the way I figured I had to be — keep myself from getting hurt by not allowing myself to feel. I got to be very good at what I do, but I also got a reputation around the base as a sort of 'ice lady.' I took pleasure in my business, and beyond that I had no pleasure. I didn't want to get to know anyone — human or otherwise — on a personal basis, because I figured that would keep me from caving in emotionally. And it seemed to work. It took a long time, but I even managed to convince myself that I had stopped loving you. . . . But then that all went out the window when I heard you say your name." She leaned toward him, and they embraced briefly.

"How did you get back up here?" Cris asked.

"Just an ordinary personnel transfer — you were a little understaffed, and we were a little over-staffed, so they asked for a few volunteers to shift bases. I figured the change of scenery wouldn't hurt, and I suppose a small part of me still held out hope that I would find out something about what had happened to you if I got back to this part of the country. But I never thought . . . I mean, what's the possibility of something like this happening?"

She put her head on his chest and clung to him. "It's so nice to be together again," she said, "but I can't wait until all of this is over. When all these monsters are gone and we can get our brains put back where they belong, we can pick up where we left off."

"Yeah," Cris said eagerly, as his mind filled with visions of Maura's slim, seductive body.

"Hey, you two," John broke in. "How about showing a little respect for someone who's—"

"I know, I know," Cris laughed. "Someone who's been on, shall we say, an unfulfilled mission for the last four years."

"That's a good way of saying it. Oh, how I long for the day when I can put my—"

"Careful, lieutenant. There's a lady present."

John cut off the rest of his sentence with an audible sigh. The three of them settled back and rode in relaxed silence for the next couple of hours, ending when Tony slowly brought the truck to a halt.

18

April 26, 2036

Nora vividly remembered the way Cris had cried the night he had first told her about the fiancée he had lost during the xenoborgs' initial invasion. His passionate description of the beautiful young woman who had stolen his heart left little doubt in Nora's mind that he would have a hard time finding someone to replace her if and when their world ever returned to normal. Nora's heart had ached for her son that night, as it had several times before and after. She wondered if his life would ever be anything but a day-to-day, fruitless exercise in survival. For even if they were fortunate enough to be able to wipe the intruders off the face of the earth, then what?

What would there be left on the devastated planet for the shattered survivors? How would her son, and others like him, recover from the trauma they had experienced during the initial invasion and the months that followed it? How would Cris ever find it possible to allow himself to invest his feelings in anything permanent when almost everyone he had ever loved and cherished had been taken from him with such terribly gruesome force?

So it had been with no small amount of gratitude and thanksgiving that Nora had wished her son and his fiancée a safe journey when they had left the complex a short time ago. It had been with the greatest of motherly love that Nora had looked on as her son and his lover were joyfully reunited shortly before taking off on their joint mission. She would have found it hard to believe that such joy and happiness could still be found in this war-torn world of hers — until now. That one, significant lovers' reunion had restored in Nora the hope she had lost a long time ago.

She knew now that no matter what her son had to face in the future, at least he would have some semblance of normalcy in his life. For although he and Maura might never again experience the same kind of relationship they had known during more pleasant days, the most important aspect of their love remained intact. Their human hearts may be in bodies thousands of miles apart, but the parts of Cris Holman and Maura Woolsey that really melded them together were packed tightly inside their cybernetic chests.

At least they had memories of what it had been like to love as completely as a man or a woman could. And now they had each other, as fully as they did then, even if the manifestations were much different. Nora wished she had such memories of intimate times with John, to help sustain her at times like this. But that wish didn't spoil her new-found happiness.

Nora had said goodbye to Cris about the same time she had said hello — and goodbye — to Maura. The young lovers had left directly on their trip to North Dakota, along with the man she loved and the other young man she had grown to love as a surrogate son. She always smiled, at least inwardly, when she thought of Tony Minelli. Happy-go-lucky Tony, who had probably been responsible for keeping Cris from going off the deep end in the first several weeks following the invasion. The kind of person any mother would be proud to claim. Nora laughed now as she also thought that Tony was the kind of person who would probably also try any mother's patience. But, oh, how easy he was to love. . . .

Nora's whole consciousness was filled with love and caring at the moment. Love for John that she had tried to deny for years; for Cris, whom she had been forced to love from afar throughout almost his entire childhood; for her son's — as well as her own — friend, who always knew how to make her smile; and for this stranger, whom Nora had come to love through her son's description of her long before they had met.

There had been no time to talk; no time for Maura to explain how she had managed to escape that first, awful onslaught of xenoborgs. No time for anything but tears and shouts of joy. No time for Nora to tell the young woman who had won her son's heart, in her own words, just how much Cris had missed Maura during their many months of separation.

But that didn't matter right now. There would be plenty of time for getting to know each other later, Nora thought as she left the loading deck and headed in the direction of the laboratory. She was confident and quietly ebullient because she *had* taken the time, just one fleeting second just after she had said goodbye to John, to make the decision she had agonized over for so long. And now she could hardly wait to tell him. When John returned, she would accept his offer of marriage. And they would wait as long as it took — forever, if necessary — to consummate the love that had blossomed so naturally and wonderfully between them despite the most unnatural of circumstances that surrounded it.

Nora pushed open the door leading into her lab and was surprised at the effort it took. It felt so heavy and hard to move that she assumed she must be even more tired than usual. She had been tired for as long as she could remember, and today was no different in that respect. But it was a different *kind* of tired. . . .

She was practically exhausted, but she still felt relaxed despite the fact that all of the people she loved were about to undertake their most dangerous mission yet. She felt more comfortable than usual under such tense circumstances because, somewhere inside, Nora Whitaker knew they would return safely. She was counting on it.

She was bursting with pride and happiness, and figured that the tiredness she felt right now came from a feeling of being tranquilized, subdued. She was feeling good about her future, the decision she had made, and what the future held for the people she loved, and all of that made her feel at peace. Yet an undercurrent of excitement surged through her system, making it almost impossible for her to contain all of the feelings and emotions, hopes and desires that she was feeling at this moment. It was a contradiction, a strange mixture of emotions, but one that she chose to savor instead of worrying about.

Before John, Cris, Tony and Maura reached their destination, before she would begin to help Traynor as one of the monitors of "Project Chase Into Space," she and Higgins would have performed their first brain transplant reversal, using what was left of R-9, the crazed cyborg whose human name was Jeff McDonnell. She knew that even if they were able to successfully reconnect the young man's brain with his body, he would probably never again be mentally healthy. But if the operation was a success, if he at least survived, then that would mean they had taken a giant step along the road heading for the time when other cyborgs would have hope of someday returning to normal. And that would mean that she and John could . . . .

Nora Whitaker never finished that pleasurable thought. She felt a horrible stab of pain in her chest a second before she lapsed into unconsciousness. After years of being pushed to its limit, both physically and emotionally, the woman's heart simply gave out — quickly, quietly, and almost painlessly. By the time Francis Higgins entered the lab five minutes later, neither he nor anyone else could do anything to save her.

19

April 26, 2036

"What's happening, corporal?"

"It's about an hour until sunrise," said Tony, "so I've been looking for a place to hole up for the day. Lift up the canvas on the right side of the truck and tell me what you think."

At the end of a long driveway just ahead of the truck and leading away from the road were the remains of a house and a barn, bathed in soft moonlight that made them stand out against the darker surrounding land — one of the thousands of small farms that dotted the rolling hills of west central Wisconsin.

"Looks like a good spot," John said to Tony. Then he turned toward Cris and Maura, who nodded their agreement.

"Let's get a closer look," suggested Cris. "If

there's something wrong with it, we still have time to find something else before daybreak."

"Okay. You and O-33 fan out on the flanks and move up ahead of us. Take it slow, S-24, and I'll watch our backside."

Cris and Maura slipped out the back of the truck and ran ahead until they were about thirty feet away from the road and fifty yards apart on opposite sides of the one-lane dirt road that snaked up a gentle hillside toward the structures. When they were in position Cris, who was closer to the truck, motioned for Tony to bring the vehicle ahead. John pulled a flap of canvas away from the rear of the cargo bed and watched out the back of the truck.

They couldn't be too careful. The terrain in this area, and for as far around them as they could see, was convoluted and rugged, overgrown with shrubs and dead grass that stood at least three feet above ground level and sometimes as high as six or seven. It was highly unlikely that something would be lurking in the weeds, waiting to ambush them, but the thick ground cover would present a problem if they were suddenly approached by an enemy force after Tony had turned the truck onto the narrow dirt road. The truck wasn't very maneuverable or very fast in reverse, and Tony would have a difficult time getting it turned around without pulling off the road. Trying to drive through the shrubbery and grass would be unwise because the truck could get hung up on a fallen tree, a gully, or dozens of other potential obstacles — and even if it didn't hit anything, it would only be able to move very slowly in an off-road situation.

Cursing — this time to himself — about the deficiencies of the vehicle he was driving, Tony nursed the truck up the gentle, twisting incline. Meanwhile, Cris and Maura moved through the brush slowly and silently, matching the speed of the vehicle and staying diagonally ahead of it at a distance of about sixty yards. When they reached the halfway point of the quarter-mile-long driveway, they left the truck behind and moved quickly to where they could get a good look — visually and electronically — at the buildings.

Both of them were still standing, more or less, but the house in particular would never be of any use again. Maura immediately noticed that two of its four exterior walls were stripped of their wooden planking from ground level to the middle of the second floor, and the other two walls had roughly half of their planks ripped off. Old-style fiberglass insulation was hanging in tatters, and in many places the interior walls had also been gouged or chopped away, revealing the modest and now weather-beaten decorations and furnishings inside.

The barn, made almost entirely of corrugated metal, was in better shape structurally. Both of its large doors had been torn off, creating a hole large enough for a xenoborg to get through. When Cris crept up to the opening and peered inside, he was surprised at how sparse and uncluttered the interior was. The concrete floor looked as though it had been scoured clean, showing not a trace of the straw or animal waste or other organic matter that typically littered the floor of a barn. No — not scoured, Cris thought. *Licked* clean. Everything except the metal and plastic is gone. Eaten. . . .

Having ascertained that the place was not dangerous, Cris and Maura joined each other at the top of the driveway and waited for Tony, John, and the truck to make the rest of their laborious approach. If they had found any reason for caution or retreat, a quick signal would have been enough to make the truck stop in its tracks and get John and Tony started on some offensive or evasive action. But no news was good news, so they simply stood and chatted while the vehicle drew closer.

"Very eerie," Maura observed, briefly describing her examination of the house.

"To say the least," Cris concurred, telling her what he had found — or, more accurately, not found — inside the barn. "It looks to me," he said, "like this place has been visited, more than once, by xenoborgs with hearty appetites."

"Probably during the winter," Maura added, "when all the grass and greenery was covered with ice."

"Yeah. I guess if you can't scrounge up any meat or green stuff, then it's easier to rip a few planks off a house than it is to chomp on a tree."

"They'll eat anything!" she said with disgust.

"Just about, except for metal and plastic," Cris responded, rapping his knuckles on his chest. "Which is why they find us a little hard to swallow."

"I've noticed," she said. "Every time I offer one of them a bite of my lasers, it seems to get a terrible case of indigestion. The poor thing just goes all to pieces."

Cris chuckled. "I think I'm going to enjoy working with you, O-33. You're a CC after my own heart." Then they laughed out loud as the double meaning of his remark hit them at the same time.

As the truck pulled up beside them and stopped, Cris silently marveled at how drastically his life and his outlook had changed in the last few hours. He had been on missions before that he could characterize afterward as "fun." He was very close to both John and Tony. But this was different, wonderfully so. Maura filled a void for him — a void he had resigned himself to living with, but all of a sudden found it so easy to live without.

It seems like things are almost back to normal, he reflected silently. Of course, he had no way of knowing that, as one void had been filled, another one had taken its place.

*   *   *

By the time the sun's disc was half exposed above the eastern horizon, the four CCs had done everything they could to conceal their presence and disguise the truck. Tony parked it on a spot of bare ground equidistant from the house and the barn. They let the air out of two of the tires and bled the other two until they were almost flat, creating the impression that the truck had not been moved for a long time and, in fact, couldn't be driven at all right now. When they needed to get rolling again, they would simply refill the tires using the pressurized canisters they had brought along.

They took off the canvas top and emptied the cargo bed, carting all of the equipment and supplies up to the loft in the barn — which, fortunately, was connected to the ground floor by a set of metal stairs. "When somebody built this barn, they built it to last," John remarked. "Little did they know . . ."

"Little did they know it would last because it wasn't nutritious," Tony quipped, finishing the thought.

"Or that it would be a stop along the way on a journey into outer space," said Cris.

"We need to get a couple of these panels off," said John, pointing to the roof. "Sounds like a job for S-24."

"Sounds like *everything* is a job for S-24," Tony said with mock resentment as he sat down to remove the legs he had only recently installed. He moved over to where the underside of the roof met the upper part of a wall, then pulled himself hand over hand, grabbing onto the metal framework, until he was dangling from the roof about ten feet above the floor of the loft.

Holding on with one hand and using the finger-tools of his other hand, he loosened the screws that attached one roof panel to its neighbor. When all of the fasteners had been removed, Maura grabbed the lower end of the oblong panel, lifted it slightly, and turned it so she could lower it down through the hole it had been covering. After two more repetitions of the process, they had created an opening about fifteen feet square — a window through which the sun could shine down onto the solar cells they needed to recharge.

Whilo Tony and Maura moved the batteries into position beneath the hole and stowed the rest of their gear in the loft, Cris and John returned to the truck and did what they could to make it appear even more decrepit and useless than it already looked. Cris pulled the driver's and passenger's doors open and let them hang. He gathered some loose wood from around the house and placed it on and around the vehicle to make it seem as though the truck had not moved since before the house had been ravaged.

Using a branch with several twigs and a few dead leaves still attached to it, John swept the loose ground along the truck's path to remove any evidence of tire tracks. Then he began picking up handfuls of the dirt and gravel and tossing it in the air above the vehicle, trying to give it at least a thin coating of dust and sediment. Cris joined in, and when they had done the job to their satisfaction they headed back to the barn together.

"All this gadgetry," Cris said, holding his dusty hands out in front of him, "and we end up using ourselves as miniature steamshovels. I haven't played in the dirt since I . . . since I was a lot younger."

"That's what they call irony, kid. All the technology in the world doesn't make a bit of difference when the only way to get a job done is get down and get your hands dirty." He paused and looked at the deserted but still fertile landscape around them. "There will always be a place for men of the soil in this world — as soon as men like us make it possible for them to reclaim what belongs to them."

"Let's go do that, okay?"

"We're on our way, Cris. We're on our way."

Now the humans must realize they are beaten, It thought with quiet glee. They not only failed to destroy the outpost with the strongest attack they could manage, they had to watch helplessly, frustrated, while it simply flew away from them.

The Master knew much about humanity, and one thing It knew with certainty was that soon the people of this planet would crumble from within — because they could not stand frustration.

20

April 26-29, 2036

They saw signs of life only three times in the next six hours — twice when vehicles trundled past along the road in the distance, and once more when a car actually came up the dirt road and stopped within fifty feet of where they were hiding.

A man got out and looked around, craning his neck as though making his field of vision a bit larger would enable him to see something new. "Try!" urged a female voice from inside the car. The man allowed his shoulders to slump as he shuffled toward the remains of the house. He walked into the kitchen, stepping through a gaping hole in the wall. Less than two minutes later he emerged and went back toward the car at the same pace. It seemed to Cris, looking on from his vantage point in the loft, that he was moving slowly in order to save his strength — or maybe because he didn't have much left.

The man passed within a few feet of the truck on the way back but gave it only a casual glance. Maybe we fooled him, Cris thought, but then realized the man's disinterest was probably caused by a different reason. The vehicle he drove was powered by an alcohol-burning engine, while the truck, having the stubby front end characteristic of such vehicles, was obviously electrical. If there was the slightest chance that the truck contained any fuel or parts he could use, Cris told himself, he would have been all over the thing in a second.

He returned to his car, leaned his forearms on the open door window, and said resignedly, "There's nothing here. Nothing we can use."

On top of his last two words came a plaintive wail. "I'm hungry!" Cris guessed that the voice came from a child of about three or four.

The man got back in the car without a word — not because he was insensitive, Cris supposed, but because he had heard that complaint many times before and had run out of meaningful responses.

"Can't we do something for them?" Maura whispered.

"No," Cris said tenderly but firmly.

"But—"

"We don't have any more food than they do. And if we take time out to get them to a place where they can find some, we'll jeopardize our mission in more ways than one."

Maura knew all of this as well as Cris did, but Cris could tell she was clearly moved by the scene she had just witnessed — especially by the child's cry. He remembered the essence of something John had said to him a few days ago — Had it really only been that long? — and he repeated it to her, hoping it would help.

"We can't help everybody all at once," he said. "The best thing we can do is accomplish what we came out here to do — because when we succeed, people like those folks won't have to suffer any more."

"You're right. It's just hard—" Maura said.

"I know," Cris interrupted, knowing only too well what the rest of that thought contained.

As the car drove back down the dirt road, Cris felt the light touch of a hand on his shoulder. He looked back at the face of C-12, and, though it was impossible, he could swear he saw John smiling.

*　*　*

Their next visitor wandered into the area about mid-afternoon. This one, too, was looking for something to eat.

Tony, stationed where he could look out on the northern horizon, saw the xenoborg first. "Hey!" he said in a near-shout. "We've got company!"

"Quiet!" John hissed. "Everybody pair up and sit tight!" He moved from his sentry post on the west wall of the loft and joined Tony. Cris came from the southern wall to an opening facing east, where Maura was kneeling and staring intently toward the house. By stationing themselves in pairs and covering the two directions that seemed important, they minimized the amount of moving around that someone would have to do if a general order had to be conveyed quietly and quickly. Of course, this also gave each CC the opportunity to communicate directly — by whispering — with his or her partner.

"Looks like it's alone," Tony said to John. "What do you make of it?"

"Could be some kind of scout or advance guard," John speculated. "Or maybe it really is alone. We'd better hope so."

The longer they waited and watched, the more it became apparent that the xenoborg was a solitary one. The thing was moving in a gentle zig-zag through the tall grass, the bottom third of its body obscured by the mostly dead vegetation that covered the hillside. Once in a while its tentacles would dip down to examine something on the ground, but most of the time the thing held its head and its extremities above the grass, looking as though it was surveying the area or sniffing the air. It wasn't emitting any radio signals, indicating that it probably was not equipped with a communication device and therefore was not a scout traveling in advance of a larger group.

When it was about fifty yards away from the house and just about to come into Cris's and Maura's field of vision, the xenoborg stopped. The rustling noise that accompanied its movement through the grass vanished, and the resulting silence was oppressive.

"It suspects something," Cris said to Maura, his voice carrying a tone of dread even though it was barely audible.

"Just being cautious," she assured him. "Don't worry. It's going to move up, grab a snack, and keep going."

"That's optimistic."

"More than that. I . . . I *know* that's what's going to happen."

"How—?"

"Shhh!" The xenoborg had begun moving again just as Cris started to utter his question.

Apparently convinced that it had nothing to fear, the thing now shuffled on a beeline for the wreckage of the house. It disappeared out of sight behind one of the walls that was still mostly intact, and an instant later the sounds of splintering and cracking wood filled the air. Then the xenoborg moved into view again, and what Cris and Maura saw was almost as humorous as it was unsettling.

Its tentacles were wrapped around about a dozen chunks of wood ranging from three to five feet in length — bite-sized pieces. The thing found a patch of bare ground and nestled down in full view of the cyborgs who were looking on from above, looking every bit like a dog that was about to savor a bone. The tentacles opened, releasing the wood into a fairly orderly pile of scrap lumber. Then the xenoborg picked up the largest chunks one at a time, turned each one so that it pointed away from the front of its body, and slowly pushed it into its gaping mouth-hole. Now the monster looked like a sword-swallower in a circus — except that it didn't draw the "swords" back out again.

Each piece was pushed in until it disappeared from sight, and then the thing closed its mouth-hole briefly. When it opened its maw again, diges-tive juices had already begun to break down the wood into a pulpy mass that could be more easily assimilated — and, consequently, the thing had room inside its mouth for one more piece. Fifteen minutes after it sat down to its repast, the xen-oborg had consumed all the wood it had scav-enged and its hunger was apparently abated, by the quantity of foodstuff if not the quality.

When it began to move again, the thing trundled along as if in slow motion, its temporarily distended belly dragging along the ground. All of the CCs knew that the xenoborg was particularly vulnerable in this condition, with the majority of its cells given over for the moment to the task of digesting its meal.

Feeling sure that any potential danger had passed, Cris motioned for John and Tony to come to where he and Maura were crouched. All four of them watched as the xenoborg waddled away, its tentacles now drooping along the ground instead of being held out alertly in front of it.

"Just one shot . . ." Tony muttered wistfully. No one found it necessary to respond to that remark, since they knew he wouldn't be so foolish as to fire on the thing. They still couldn't be absolutely sure that other monsters weren't in the vicinity, or that this one didn't have the ability to communicate with its fellows. As much as all of them wanted to fry the monster, they knew they couldn't take even the slightest chance of being discovered.

When the thing was at a safe distance, just about to disappear over the crest of a hill to the southeast, the four of them relaxed and began to speak in normal tones of voice again.

"It seems strange to hide from one of those things," Maura observed. "I've never had to watch one walk away from me before."

"I know the feeling," said Tony, recalling the way he and Cris had been forced to avoid detection on their mission against the teleborg.

"Let's get back to it, people," John said, moving back toward his lookout station. "Still a couple of hours before we can travel again."

As Tony also moved away, Cris remembered the question he had not had a chance to finish.

"How did you know?" he asked Maura.

She knew right away what he was talking about, but she answered in a whisper, as though she was ashamed of her prediction. "I don't know *how*," she said. "I just knew. I could . . . I could see the thing sitting down to eat, and then moving away, even before it got to the house."

"I think you've been cooped up in a barn too long," Cris teased.

"Don't laugh," she said defensively, his reaction telling her that he wasn't taking her seriously. "And please don't say anything to them," she breathed, nodding toward the far end of the loft.

"You're really troubled by this, aren't you?" Cris asked tenderly.

"Wouldn't you be troubled if you could see what was going to happen right before it actually did?"

"Yeah, I'm sure I would. But if you're really good at this, maybe it could help us—"

Maura didn't give him a chance to finish.

"Don't tell the others, please," she pleaded.

"Why not?"

"I'm . . . I'm not sure what it's all about. I can't always do it when I want to, and sometimes it happens when I don't expect it. When I try to prove I can do it, just to satisfy someone else, it never works, and then I just get laughed at."

"I'm not laughing," Cris said supportively.

"You almost did when I first told you," Maura argued.

"Yeah, but, well, . . ." Cris sputtered, not quite sure what to say in his defense. He didn't put much stock in vague, extraordinary mental powers, although he had read enough about them to admit to himself that some people seemed to have abilities along those lines. But formal, structured experiments had usually been inconclusive, or their results vulnerable to critical examination; if these powers did exist, apparently they couldn't always be called up on cue. "Look. I'm sorry. I really do understand, and I won't tell a soul, okay?" Cris said, hoping to set her mind at ease.

"Hey, you two," John called out, gruff but friendly. "Break it up."

"Thanks," Maura whispered to Cris.

"Sure," he said. Then he moved back to his post, thinking that there was more to O-33 than met the eye or the ear. I guess I still have a lot to learn about her, he told himself. And there was no doubt in his mind that he was going to enjoy every single minute and every new discovery. He was so happy that she was back in his life. He had a feeling that Cris Holman's world was finally beginning to take a turn for the better . . .

* * *

The remainder of their journey to North Dakota was relatively uneventful. By skirting well around the Minneapolis-St. Paul area, they avoided the only known heavy concentration of aliens in the north central United States, and most of the terrain over which they traveled was utter wilderness.

"This is as far as we go," John said abruptly, about two hours before sunrise on April 29.

Tony pulled the truck off the road, and they once again went through the routine of breaking it down and unloading it to make it appear useless and abandoned. This time, however, they left the solar cells in the back of the truck. They were almost depleted from the last several hours of use, and they wouldn't be needed any more since the cyborgs could easily make the rest of their journey on foot. They each took a box containing some of the spare parts they might need and then set out in single file about a hundred yards apart, heading northwest.

At precisely 0530, when the sun was still just a faint glow coming from below the horizon behind them, all of them detected the signal they were expecting — a transmission, less than a second in duration, that enabled them to fix the distance and direction between them and their destination. Without needing to be told what to do, all of them veered slightly to line up their route with the source of the signal — about three miles away and just a couple of degrees north of the direction they had been taking.

The transmission came from the men who were staffing an underground missile silo, one of the few such installations in this part of the country that had escaped destruction in the first cataclysmic hours of the invasion. They knew that visitors — friendly ones — were on the way, and they had orders to broadcast a homing signal at 0530 and 2000 hours every day until the CCs showed up or until receiving a message that they had been lost en route.

"Good timing," Cris muttered to himself with satisfaction. They would be able to reach the hidden entrance to the installation and get inside before daybreak. He considered their receipt of the signal as a good omen, a sign that the rest of the mission would also come off as planned and on schedule. If all did go well, about eighteen hours from now they would be aboard a capsule atop an enormous guided missile, rocketing toward a life-or-death encounter on the fringe of outer space.

21

April 28, 2036

Frank Higgins felt less confident in what he was about to do than he had ever felt before. Maybe it was because Nora Whitaker, whom he had come to respect and admire in the short time they had been together, was no longer there to contribute her skill and her moral support. Maybe it was because her death had brutally reminded him of his own mortality. If I push too hard, he asked himself, will the same thing happen to me? As much as this project meant to him, his own survival meant more. Maybe it was because deep inside he thought that he had about one chance in a thousand of succeeding at what he was trying to accomplish.

"Damn!" Higgins cursed to himself as he scrubbed for surgery. "What's the point of going through the motions when we all know this is a lost cause?" He realized he had uttered that thought aloud when the other doctors and technicians in the room with him suddenly ceased all their conversation. Higgins just shook his head and went about his business. They're all blind optimists, he thought sadly. They really think they can beat this thing that's come to do them in.

He continued to prepare to observe and direct the surgical procedure that was due to begin momentarily, while those around him resumed their conversations. Only one person, Aaron Traynor, approached the tired old man.

"I'm feeling a bit defeated myself, Frank. It's a natural thing to feel after losing someone you love."

Higgins gave Traynor an appreciative look, his feeling one of kinship and shared loss. "Hell, Aaron, I hardly knew her, but . . . ."

"I know. She was quite a person. She had an amazing amount of talent and inner strength. And I will personally miss her more than I can even say." Traynor felt a tremor in his lower lip and quickly bit down hard to stop it.

Higgins took a deep breath and closed his eyes, as though he was trying to block out everything around him. When he spoke, it was with restrained anger that grew more obvious with each bitter word. "The thing is, she dreamed of the day when she would be able to put her arms around her own flesh and blood, you know? It was one of the few things she wanted." Higgins paused, still trying to keep his anger in check. But his effort failed as he loudly blurted out, "It sounds so damn trite, but Nora Whitaker was a person who devoted her life to helping her fellow man. And she was convinced she was within reach of finally getting a well-deserved rest, of living the kind of life she lost so many years ago. But what she didn't realize was that it would all be in vain — just like whatever we do here today will be in vain. Even if we do succeed, what difference is it going to make when those aliens have finally killed us off?"

Higgins's voice had reached about as high a pitch as it could reach. Not one person in the room tried to argue with him, partly because they didn't want to upset him further and partly because, for all they knew, he was right.

Traynor was the first to speak. "Look, Frank. We all know the score. None of us knows whether we'll be around a year from now, a week from now, or even a day from now. But we're working on the assumption that there is a chance we'll beat this thing. Without that hope, without that blind conviction we all tend to doubt from time to time, there would be no point in continuing to live.

"We *are* still alive, Frank, and those of us who believe the old saying that where there's life, there's hope, will continue to hope for a better tomorrow. And as long as we keep doing that, as long as we refuse to give up, whatever the hell it is out there that wants us gone is, at the very least, going to have to put up one hell of a fight before it gets its way!" Traynor gently squeezed Higgins's shoulder and then added, "Now c'mon, doc. You're due in surgery."

* * *

Francis Higgins pulled the plastic gloves off his hand and dropped them in the nearest waste receptacle. Traynor, who had come into the room after the conclusion of the surgical procedure, pulled off his own gloves and facemask and sighed a long, tired sigh.

"So how does it feel to be a hero, Francis?" Traynor asked, allowing a broad smile to dominate his facial features.

Higgins rubbed his tired eyes with the palms of both hands and then blinked hard to focus. He felt a strange combination of elation and despair, and he didn't want the despair to take over and ruin this moment of triumph. But he had to face the facts. "You realize," he said to Traynor, "that just because the surgery went as planned, that doesn't mean we're home free yet. It'll be several days before we are sure that the procedure did not cause any brain damage. And that will be difficult to determine, considering the mental state of the subject when he underwent the operation."

Having worked the pessimism out of his system

for the moment, he paused for a moment and continued. "However, it could have been a lot worse. The man is alive — and, frankly, I didn't expect him to come through. What we have done here, whether it turns out to be a complete success or not, gives us every reason to believe that we have come closer to our goal. Some day soon we might solve the puzzle for once and for all."

"What this means, Francis, is that you and Nora did one hell of a job and you should be proud." Traynor said, still smiling from ear to ear.

"I only wish Nora had been here to see it," Higgins said, his cloudy mood taking over again.

"I know," Traynor agreed, the broad smile suddenly slipping into a solemn frown.

"Have either Crls or John been informed of her death yet?" Higgins asked.

"No."

"But she was going to be monitoring some of that. They're expecting to be able to communicate with her. How are you going to keep them from finding out?"

"We're going to fake it the best we can. That's all we can do. If we tell them now, we may be putting the mission in jeopardy."

"And if you wait until after they've left the ground, you may never have to worry about having to tell them at all," Higgins said soberly.

22

April 29, 2036

There was nothing around him for as far as John could see — nothing but wasteland, both of the natural and manmade sort. The only feature that looked like it hadn't been here for decades, if not longer, was a bombed-out concrete structure and the remains of a few outbuildings sprinkled around it. He didn't expect to see any obvious signs of life or activity, but somehow he had expected more than this. . . .

He stopped about two hundred yards away from the wreckage, turned around, and motioned for Tony, who was next in line, to join him. S-24 passed the signal along, and the four of them started to close ranks.

"This has to be the place," John said softly to Tony.

"Yeah," said Tony, "but it can't be — unless somebody got here before we did."

Cris and Maura were equally befuddled and hesitant when they came up to join the group. The four of them had been told that the location of their destination would be "obvious" to them as they approached it. Certainly they had tracked on the homing signal correctly; certainly there was nowhere else within miles from where the signal could have come. But what would they be getting into if they went closer?

"Okay," John said decisively. "Fan out and approach with caution. . . . Wait! Hit the deck!"

The four of them dropped the boxes they were carrying and flattened immediately. They had no cover to duck behind, but at least they would present smaller targets if they were prone.

Cris had picked up on what John perceived in virtually the same instant, and he assumed the others had heard it too — the unmistakable sounds of movement coming from behind a section of concrete wall on the side of the building they were facing. Someone, or something, was in the rubble, moving under its own power, and the CCs weren't going to go any closer until they identified it.

Then another sound, a more welcome one, reached their hypersensitive auditory sensors. It was the voice of a man, speaking just loud enough to be heard across the distance that separated him from the cyborgs: "You must be the chasers."

The man repeated the sentence twice more, each time at a slightly louder volume, as if trying to be sure that he would be heard. John delivered the second half of the password combination. "And you must be the spacers."

"Yep. Welcome to our humble abode," the man roplied.

The CCs got to their feet and covered the distance between themselves and the wreckage in a matter of seconds. Just as they pulled up alongside the remains of a wall, a man dressed in military fatigues stepped out from behind it. "This way," he said briskly.

Ho followod a oonvolutod path ovcr and through the rubble, heading farther away from the exterior walls all the time. The cyborgs followed, actually having a hard time keeping up with him in certain spots. Then the man stopped in front of an enormous piece of twisted, pitted metal, grabbed the edge of it, and pulled.

"Let me . . ." John was about to offer his assistance, but stopped speaking when he saw the panel pivot toward them. He stepped forward, grabbed the edge, and discovered that the panel was not made of metal but rather some sort of lightweight plastic that had been disguised to look like part of the wreckage.

On the other side of the door was a small landing and a set of steps leading down — as it turned out, a *lot* of steps. The man got out a pocket flashlight, started to descend, and the visitors followed. "Elevator's been broken for quite a while now," he said laconically, "and we just haven't had the time to get it fixed. But we figured you husky types wouldn't mind."

After they passed through a door that Cris estimated was at least three hundred feet below ground level and several hundred feet laterally from where they had begun their descent, he became immediately and solemnly amazed at what he found inside. "Wow," he said under his breath.

"That doesn't even begin to describe it!" Tony exclaimed.

They were inside some sort of control room filled with a hodgepodge of electronic equipment — monitor screens, banks of lights and switches, and enough seats to accommodate a dozen people. Five of the seats were occupied when they arrived, and everyone's attention was fixed, directly or indirectly, on the biggest conversation piece Cris Holman had ever seen.

Only a small part of it was visible on a monitor screen on the far wall, but even that was impressive beyond description — a massive, gleaming cylinder of metal, a tribute to man's technology and his tenacity.

"So that's what we'll be riding in," said Maura.

"Riding on top of, actually." The response came from a middle-aged man who had risen from his seat and come over to greet them. "My name is

Mallough," he said. "Supposedly the one in charge, although we don't pay too much attention to rank around here." Cris looked more closely at the man, then glanced around the room. Indeed, all of them were dressed in identical, nondescript uniforms and none of them wore any insignia.

"That's just fine," John said. "Neither do we — right, folks?"

"Oh, no, sir!" Tony chirped. "Whatever you say, sir."

John sighed. "The army just isn't what it used to be." A second after making the remark, John wished he had thought twice before speaking. An uneasy silence hung over the group for a moment, with no one sure what to do or say next. Cris was grateful when Mallough broke the tension.

"You folks had better check in," he said. "The people at home will be glad to hear from you."

"And vice versa," Cris said.

Communication from here to Manitowoc and back again was virtually instantaneous despite the need for secrecy, thanks to the computers on both ends of the link that took an outgoing message, condensed it electronically, and sent it out on an everchanging set of frequencies. An incoming message was handled in reverse fashion, unscrambled in milliseconds and then displayed on a monitor screen. Under the circumstances, it was the next best thing to actually talking with someone, although both the sender and receiver understood that messages had to be kept as short and efficient as possible.

Cris took the output lead that Mallough offered him, opened a small panel in his upper chest, and plugged it into the socket inside. This would enable him to transmit information by simply thinking it. Instead of sending the message out through his own transmitting antenna, his internal computer would route it into the output lead and send it to the base antenna on the surface. At the same time, the essence of what he was "saying" would appear on the screen interspersed with the incoming information.

Cris's internal computer received an impulse that indicated the channel was open. He started sending immediately. Roughly a minute later, Manitowoc knew that they had arrived safely with no breach of security along the way, and that, according to Mallough, the rocket that would carry the CCs would be ready for launch in about twelve hours, which meant that the preliminary phase of "Project Chase" could proceed on schedule.

Cris learned that most of the other CC teams involved in the mission had also reached their destinations safely within the last few hours, so the operation would go off at full scale or nearly so. At roughly the same time that Cris, John, Maura, and Tony would be rocketing into space, a dozen other Cyborg Commando teams from bases around the world would be going up to assume different orbits.

The intent was to throw a lethal screen of firepower up around the planet, so that any teleborg trying to escape death by leaving Earth would find death waiting for it in the airless void.

Mallough, having scanned the exchange of information on the screen as it took place, was beaming when the check-in ended. "All right," he said with cheerful briskness. "It looks like everything is go, so I'd better get these people started on final prep."

"Something's not right," Cris said soberly as Mallough moved away from the group.

"What?" John asked anxiously. "Nothing in the message . . ."

"No, not that. Didn't you notice? I was talking to Traynor."

"And?"

"And he's only supposed to be on duty from 1200 to 2400. My . . . Nora was supposed to be our contact at this time of day."

"So they swapped," said Tony nonchalantly. "What difference does it make?"

"But everything was so precisely planned. Why the change?"

"Your mother has other things to worry about," suggested John. "Maybe she got hung up in surgery, maybe she needed to get some rest. Heck, she's got a lot of pull — maybe she just decided she wanted to see us off instead of taking the morning shift."

"I'm sure it's nothing to worry about, Cris," said Maura.

"Heck," Tony quipped, "he worries if he *doesn't* have anything to worry about."

"Okay, you guys," Cris said, holding up his hands in surrender. "Three to one. You're right. It's probably nothing at all."

* * *

They had the run of the place for the next few hours — not that they could run very far. Without needing to talk it over first, all of them decided that the best thing they could do for themselves was to keep busy mentally and thereby avoid dwelling on the danger in what they were about to undertake. Each of them strolled casually around the control room, watching the technicians go through their arcane but interesting rituals of checking, double-checking, and usually triple-checking all the systems that would get the huge missile off the ground and bring their capsule back down safely.

This installation was one of twenty-three underground launch sites around the world that had managed to escape obliteration. Like the other ones that were still operational, it had formerly housed a missile armed with thermonuclear devices — a weapon designed by man to be used against other men. Apparently because the xenoborgs did not want to — or could not — contend with man's arsenal of "hot" bombs and the resultant fallout, they had used high-intensity lasers to cripple or destroy most of the launch sites almost immediately.

But a few of the missiles and the technology needed to operate them came through the onslaught unscathed. For the last several months, crews had been working painstakingly and under enormous hardship to convert each weapon into a missile that could carry a payload — living or otherwise — into orbit. Exactly what those payloads would consist of had not been decided at the time, but it was generally agreed that a worthwhile purpose could be found for the missiles once they were ready to go up.

Such a purpose became apparent after the abortive attempt to kill the teleborg near Milwaukee. The word went out and around the planet in a matter of little more than an hour, and with speed born of desperation a plan — the only workable plan, really — was formed and put into motion.

Thirteen four-member teams of Cyborg Commandos embarked from their bases scant hours later, almost simultaneously, each heading for a missile site that could be reached in three or four days of overland travel.

As each CC base received word that its "chasers" had arrived safely, two-member squads would start going out on missions identical to the one Cris and Tony had undertaken.

Between 1700 and 1900 today, the big guns would go into action. First, a group of rockets would be launched — special missiles with the capability of eluding electronic tracking systems — to knock out the monitoring satellites that the enemy had placed in orbit. Shortly thereafter, thirteen missiles would emerge from their cocoons and take the chasers aloft.

Then air strikes would commence against the teleborgs that had been incapacitated — and this time, it would not be bad news if the attacks "failed" and caused the creatures to take flight. Each capsule would remain aloft until its orbit started to deteriorate, and would blast every teleborg it could find in the meantime.

It was the first time in the history of man's fight to recover his planet that a truly worldwide effort was being undertaken — and, as large-scale plans go, a more ambitious one could not have been devised by the most imaginative military thinkers. Nobody was making any guarantees or even going so far as to make a qualified prediction of success. But the plan could work, if all the parts came together just right.

*   *   *

"Shit! There it goes again!"

John couldn't help but overhear that muttered curse as he came up behind a technician who was oblivious to his presence. "There goes what?" asked C-12 in a conversational tone.

The man jumped, looked over his shoulder at John, then stammered out a response.

"It's . . . We've . . . There's a problem with the generator in the capsule," he said softly. "We've rewired it three times in the last day, but it burns out whenever we run it for more than a couple of hours at a time."

"Which means?" John asked, suspecting what the answer would be.

"If we fix it again and don't test it, the capsule might have electrical power for only about five hours once we got it up — two hours before the generator goes, and three more before the batteries run dry."

"We can accomplish a lot in five hours," John said. Mallough came up beside him in time to hear that remark.

"But," Mallough said, cutting in before the technician could speak, "you wouldn't be able to return without power to operate the re-entry guidance systems. In that case, the best we could do would be to send you up for one or two orbits, and then you'd have to get back down in a hurry."

"Hardly worth the trip," John observed. Then a thought struck him. "Would it make a difference if I could get you another source of power, another set of batteries?"

"Yes," said Mallough. "But you can't . . ." he

continued, gesturing toward the part of John's torso where his power supply was located.

"Oh, not me. I was thinking of the buggy we rode in on. We left a good set of solar cells in it. I can get 'em and be back before you can say 're-entry guidance systems.' How about it?"

"You can't go alone!" This came from Tony, who had noticed the conversation and moved within earshot as John was making his offer. "It's daytime. If you're seen—"

"If one of us can be spotted, two of us can be spotted twice as easily."

"Yeah, but—"

"No buts, corporal. We don't have time to debate it, and there's nothing to discuss anyway. And if either of them tries to follow me"— John nodded toward the adjoining chamber, where Cris and Maura were getting a close-up look at the missile —"I will hold you personally responsible for opening your big mouth."

"Let him go," said Mallough. "It's the best chance we've got. And he's right — we don't have much time."

Tony stood silently and watched as John and Mallough crossed the room together. The man opened the door leading to the stairway, and John slipped through the opening and disappeared. A second later, Tony whirled and ran for the missile room.

23

April 29, 2036

"He's gone!" Tony shouted as he burst into the chamber where Cris and Maura were standing.

"What?" They whirled and asked the question simultaneously.

"John! He's gone back up!" In a frenzied babble, Tony spent the next minute explaining what he knew about what John was trying to do. A short time later, Cris and Maura had cornered Mallough and gotten the full story.

"So why are we standing here?" Tony was still frantic. "Do I have to go by myself?"

"Nobody's going anywhere," Cris said, trying to keep the anxiety out of his voice. "John made the right decision. We have to have those batteries, and it's not a two-man job."

In truth, Cris didn't believe his own words. He

wished John had taken a partner — preferably Cris himself — because he knew that C-12 wouldn't be able to defend himself very well while carrying a double armload of batteries. But there was nothing to be done for it now; John was certainly a good distance away from the launch site already, and it would be pointless to try to catch him. But . . .

"Tell you what," Cris said after a short pause. "I'll go up and keep a watch for him from the edge of the wreckage. If he gets within sensor range and it looks like he's in trouble, I'll—"

"No, Cris," Maura interrupted. "I'll go, and I'll take a box of spare parts. If he does get in trouble, I can help him in more ways than you can."

Cris sighed. "I can't argue with that logic."

"Then let's cut the chatter and move it!" Tony practically shouted. Ten minutes later, Maura had selected the equipment she was most likely to need and was ready to head up the stairs.

"Be careful," Cris said to her softly but firmly. "And that's an order. If you—"

"Don't worry, Cris. I can take care of myself."

"I hope so," he murmured as the door shut behind her. "I hope so."

* * *

All of the CCs had kept their use of electronic aids to a strict minimum for the last several days, in the interest of both conserving power and keeping their existence secret from any sensor-carrying xenoborgs within range. But John knew he couldn't afford that sort of caution now. Xenoborgs were much more mobile and much more aggressive during the day than they were at night; he pessimistically expected to run across at least a small group of them on this excursion, and he needed to operate his sensors and receptors at full power and maximum sensitivity to give himself as much warning as possible if any creatures did come within range.

It was a good tactic, the same decision anyone else should have made in the same circumstances. John Edwards was perhaps the oldest living Cyborg Commando in the world — in terms of the time his brain had spent inside an artificial body — and he was an expert at knowing when and how to make best use of the powers and abilities of that body. When he was feeling good about his situation, as he was now, he always thought he was the best man for any job that only a CC could accomplish.

And he was right . . . up to a point. Up to the point where his body stopped doing what his brain told it to.

Sometimes it's impossible to tell, even under close examination, if a light bulb is about to burn out. A contact point on a switch can slowly erode, unnoticed, for months or years, until the two ends of the connection no longer meet and a problem "suddenly" crops up. In the case of Cyborg Commando C-12, the problem spot was a microscopically small portion of one of the printed circuit boards that controlled the movement of his legs. The defect had never been detected, or even searched for, in refit examinations, because John's mechanical extremities had always worked perfectly in performance tests, and no trouble of this sort had ever cropped up in a Cyborg Commando. Then again, few if any cybernetic bodies were as old as John's.

If the four "chasers" from Manitowoc had made their journey to North Dakota on foot, John's legs would have given out after a few miles — and Maura would have been able to repair the damage or replace the defective part in a matter of minutes. But C-12 had spent most of the last four days riding in the back of a truck, not having to use his legs. And now, when he needed them . . .

"Damn!"

That was the first word John had uttered since leaving the launch site, and he said it for a very good reason. All of a sudden his right leg felt stiff, and it was getting less responsive by the second. He knew right away that something was wrong, but he hoped it wouldn't turn out to be too serious. He had the truck in sight, a mere quarter-mile away, and from what he could see and sense the vehicle had not been disturbed since they had abandoned it.

All I have to do is get there and hole up, he thought. If I don't get back in, oh, a half-hour or so, someone will come out after me. Just have to keep moving. . . .

But moving was difficult, and it quickly became impossible. Thirty seconds later, his right leg went dead and his left was responding as though he was wading through hip-deep mud. He came to a halt, hoping against hope that if he rested, a renewed surge of power would flow into his lower extremities.

Then he saw them.

Nine bulbous, unnatural shapes came into view at virtually the same time, appearing on the crest of a ridge that was about half a mile away from where John stood. On the featureless terrain, even the very tops of their grayish-white bodies stood out in stark relief against the dark ground and the pale blue sky.

They, or at least one of them, noticed John a couple of seconds after he had detected them. Their immediate response was to start moving faster and farther apart — spreading themselves out, he supposed, so that he wouldn't be able to pick them all off in short order. They spent the next several minutes forming into a wide arc, each one several hundred yards from its neighbor, and keeping their distance.

Sizing me up, John thought. Waiting for me to make the first move. . . . He chuckled silently at his unintentional joke, then tested his left leg. His brain told it to move, and he could almost feel the minuscule surge of electricity flow down, down — to a place just above the hip joint, where it stopped. The leg had gone dead, just like the other one, and he was now unable to put one foot in front of the other.

But he was not without resources, both mental and mechanical. By thrusting his upper body forward and overbalancing, he tipped himself and fell into a prone position, cushioning his fall with his hands. He rested his upper body on his elbows, pointing his arms forward, and panned his gaze from left to right to take in the line of monsters. They moved excitedly for a few seconds after he dropped down, but quickly ascertained that the movement was not immediately threatening to them.

"Come on, you bastards!" John growled. "You're holding the cards — play 'em!" But the standoff continued for an interminable few minutes. John considered each of the few options available to him, but dismissed them in turn. Firing on the monsters was pointless; he might take out two or three, but the others would scatter and eventually surround him — and when they found out he was practically defenseless against an attack from his rear, they would waste no time making use of that knowledge. Trying to move by pulling himself along on his elbows would be even worse; they were probably too stupid to see it as a trick, and would instead assume the truth — that he was disabled. Sending a message for help was probably pointless, since (damn!) he had insisted that everyone else stay inside, and if he did use his radio there was a good chance that the xenoborgs would interpret the tactic as an offensive gesture or an act of desperation. Either way, it would probably incite them to attack.

Then the monsters made his decision for him. They still didn't move, but John's receptors suddenly picked up radio signals being transmitted by the xenoborg in the center of the line. Was it calling for reinforcements? Issuing an order to attack? Either way, it was time for John to stop being passive and take some action himself.

He turned on his transmitter and began broadcasting a signal for help. Then he aimed his forearms toward the two xenoborgs he could target on most easily and fired.

Both of the laser blasts hit what they aimed at, and even from such a long distance John could see the vapor rise from the holes he had sliced through the bodies. The two monsters turned and headed for the safety of the other side of the hill, and for a second John felt a glimmer of hope. If he could scorch each of them and get all of them to turn tail, he could buy some time . . . time for someone to respond to his distress call.

He pivoted his upper body awkwardly, wishing

he could get rid of his dead legs instead of having to drag them along, and tried to sight on another pair of monsters. As he fired again — one hit and one miss this time — he glimpsed something out of the corner of his eye that made him freeze.

The xenoborg at the extreme left end of the line was raising a weapon — a laser. Before he could scrabble around to get the creature in his line of fire, a searing blast of light angled into the ground a few feet away from him, throwing up small chunks of dirt and gravel that rained down on his body. Just before he got the attacker in his sights, another blast hit the ground — on his other side.

John got off a shot that hit the monster firing from his left. A fraction of a second later, another laser shot from his right caught him just above the neck. The blast burned out some of his sensors but did not cause him to lose consciousness.

Now at least three other monsters with weapons had joined in the assault. John, virtually immobile, took one hit after another, absorbing ten times the damage it would have taken to kill a human being. He remained alive and aware of what was happening, even though he couldn't do anything about it.

Then, being merciful without meaning to, one of the monsters hit John again. This shot took him in the chest, hitting his organic brain and his internal computer at virtually the same time.

On the desolate plains of North Dakota, alone and helpless, John Edwards died.

24

April 29, 2036

"It's been too long," Cris said, his voice rising in volume at the end of the statement.

"About an hour," Mallough said, as though he too suspected something had gone wrong.

"Yeah, and he could have — should have — been back by now." That came from Tony. "I'm going up."

"No, I'm—"

"Your partner would have let us know if something was wrong," Mallough argued.

"Unless she's in trouble too!" Cris was becoming almost frantic.

"Then I'll send someone out to check on her," Mallough cut in firmly. "But I can't let either one of you leave. Without at least two of you, we can't send anyone up—"

"Who says you can stop me?" Cris fumed. "I lost Maura once and I'm not going to lose her again!" He took off for the door leading to the seemingly endless set of stairs. But before he even got to it, the door opened and Maura stepped through. As soon as the door closed behind her, she let the case of parts fall to the floor with a loud crash and bent over, putting her face in her hands.

Cris rushed to her side with Tony hot on his heels. "What happened?" Cris asked, taking her by the shoulders.

"Oh, Cris, I'm afraid John's—" The looks on Cris and Tony's faces stopped her from finishing her sentence.

"What?" Tony asked sharply, dreading the answer but needing to hear it all the same, just in case the terrible thoughts that were going through his mind weren't true. "John's what?" This time he nearly screamed the question.

Maura looked up at them and then, quietly and compassionately, she uttered the only word they didn't want to hear. "Dead. He's dead." And then she collapsed emotionally, releasing the tension, horror, and sadness she had been storing up for months.

In the next few heart-wrenching minutes, Cris and Tony managed to coax Maura back to a semblance of calmness and get most of the information they needed out of the distraught woman. She told them about picking up a distress call after she had been outside for a while. "It had to be John," she said between sobs. "Who else could it be?" They let the question go unanswered.

"But before I could do anything about it, the signal stopped. No signoff, no fadeout — it just . . . stopped."

"Maybe his transmitter just broke down," Tony said, searching for a ray of hope. "Maybe he's—"

"No." Maura's voice was suddenly even and firm. "I looked out in the direction he had gone. I stared as hard as I could. And then I . . . I saw him. Lying on the ground. Broken, not moving — with monsters all around him!"

"You saw him?" Tony asked, barely able to keep from screaming the question. "Why the hell didn't you—"

Cris cut his friend off before he had a chance to verbally attack Maura. "You don't understand," he said. "She saw him . . . in her mind."

"What the hell—"

"Listen to him, Tony. He's right. That's what I meant. Sometimes I can see things inside me, and every time I've had a real strong impression, a clear image, it's turned out to be true.

"I saw a Cyborg Commando on the ground, with xenoborgs circling around, pushing and pulling on his body. Who else could it have been?" she concluded, repeating her earlier question. This time, as before, no one bothered to give the obvious answer.

"Do you expect me to buy this shit?" Tony sputtered. "I say we go the hell out there and see for ourselves"

"There's no longer any reason to do that." Those quietly spoken words came from Mallough, who had left the room when Maura broke down. "We have confirmation. Pilots on security surveillance have reported the presence of a cluster of xenoborgs a few miles south of here. They also spotted the . . . the body of a Cyborg Commando."

No one spoke for several minutes, but the sound of soft weeping, coming from the usually jovial Tony Minelli, filled the chamber.

Mallough cleared his throat uncertainly and broke the silence. "I'm very sorry," he said with genuine sincerity.

"We shouldn't have let him go," Tony said, his feelings of guilt and grief almost too much to bear.

"I don't understand," Cris said quietly. "I worked with the man. He was the best. There's no way he would have let an army of xenoborgs overtake him. Something must have gone wrong."

"I'm sure we'll find out what happened when the . . . body . . . is examined. But in the meantime, and without meaning to sound callous, we have to get on with this mission," Mallough said.

"Yeah. We do." Cris's voice was steely cold, his mind filled with the same hatred and determination he had first felt more than a year ago, before he became a Cyborg Commando and after his loved ones had been taken from him by the invaders. An overwhelming desire for revenge filled his consciousness, just as it had then.

It occurred to him, as though he was observing himself from a distance, that he was not having a difficult time dealing with the fact of John's death. Then he identified the reason. All of them, all the CCs and the rest of the human race as well, were living on the edge every minute of their lives. They had all come to realize, at least subconsciously, that any one of them could be killed at any time. Somehow, that realization made tragedy easier to deal with when it happened.

But Cris Holman was not giving up — far from it. He and his friends would live on the edge for at least a while longer, and for as long as he survived he would be a ruthless, vicious team leader, pushing his comrades and himself to do everything they could to annihilate the teleborgs and xenoborgs. Now I have one more reason to want to kill every last one of them, Cris thought — not as a way of cheapening John's death, but as his way of giving it significance and meaning. You're in pretty good company, pal, he thought, as the faces of his father, stepmother, and sister came into his mind. Give them my love — and save a little for yourself, too. . . .

"Cris." Tony, now semi-composed, spoke his name as Maura touched his arm, both acts bringing him back to the here and now.

"Yeah."

"I have an idea," Tony continued. "When the batteries start to run down, we can bleed power from my leg unit. I won't need it anyway."

"That's no replacement for a set of fresh batteries," Mallough cautioned.

"But it'll buy us some time, right?"

"Maybe enough for another orbit, but we can't be sure," the man guessed.

"Enough to make the trip worthwhile?" Maura asked.

"If we get up there and kill even one of those creatures — one that no one else could have gotten to — then the trip will have been worthwhile. We can't do a thing sitting in here, that's for sure."

"It's risky, but if you're willing—"

"We're willing!" all three cyborgs said in unrehearsed unison, startling each other and causing Mallough to smile.

"I had a feeling you'd feel that way. So what are we waiting for?"

* * *

The capsule had a jury-rigged look about it, but beneath the mismatched collection of gadgetry visible on the surface, the vessel was a technological marvel considering what the technicians had to work with.

Beginning with the casing at the top of the cylinder that had formerly contained a bundle of nuclear warheads, the engineers and electricians stripped it to its frame and installed inside it all the trappings necessary to carry men, or cyborgs, into outer space and enable them to maneuver the vessel once they had achieved orbit.

Tony would be the navigator, since only he — minus his leg unit — could fit into the cramped quarters adjacent to the capsule's guidance systems. The other members of the team sat around the base of the blunt cone-shaped capsule, where three more spacious seats formed an equilateral triangle facing outward. On this trip, of course, only two of the seats would be occupied. The CCs' oversized bodies fit into these stations comfortably, since all of the capsule's onboard hardware had been removed; the passengers would be bringing their own.

In front of each gunner's seat was a wide-angle viewport, and beneath that was an open slot through which the CC would extend his or her forearms prior to opening fire. Once the capsule was up, its inside would be as airless as the space through which it traveled — but that was perfectly all right, since Cyborg Commandos could operate in a vacuum as easily as they could in the atmosphere. They had to beware of the bitter cold temperatures, however; if the hydraulics and other moving parts in their joints stiffened up or froze, they would be in big trouble. In anticipation of this problem, the workers had installed heating coils on the inside of the capsule walls. Those would help to keep the temperature within a tolerable range, and each CC would also use internal heating systems to raise his or her body temperature for as long as necessary.

Manufacturing all that heat consumed energy, of course, and that was where the batteries came in. Almost from the minute the missile left its launching pad, the capsule's power supply would be taxed to its limit as it provided not only heat but the electrical energy needed to operate the vessel's guidance systems. The batteries would not be replenished once the generator gave out — as everyone had to assume it would — and from then on, the only source of external power would be the high-capacity but relatively small batteries in S-24's leg unit. That was the power they would rely on to complete their last orbit and operate the re-entry guidance systems that, if they worked properly, would bring the capsule down in Lake Michigan — a few miles from where the strange, tragic odyssey of Cris, Maura, and Tony had begun.

With minutes to spare before they had to vacate the area and make final launch preparations, the technicians finally finished crafting a lead that Tony could use to connect his leg unit to the power outputs leading from the batteries. All three CCs had received a crash course —"Don't take that literally," Mallough had said— in what they could expect during liftoff and re-entry, and had been shown how to work the few manual controls they would be required to operate.

Cris had no chance to devote much thought to what was about to happen, because he still had one duty to perform before liftoff. Mallough had his internal computer and transmitter patched into the launch site's communication facilities, and Cris made his second and last mission status report to Manitowoc.

He was dreading it, because he didn't want to be the one to tell his mother about John — certainly not over such a long distance and in such an impersonal way. Then he was almost relieved, but unsettled at the same time, to discover that he was again "talking" to Traynor instead of Nora.

Traynor gave Cris the go-ahead to implement the final phase of the operation — not that he could have prevented the launch anyway. He took the news of John's death with what seemed like cool disinterest, judging by his response: "Mission is still a go for three." Cris was initially angry at the attitude he thought was conveyed by those words, but he settled down quickly, realizing that everyone had to be all business at this point; the time for letting emotions go would come later, if it came at all. Cris asked Traynor not to inform his mother of John's death and received a one-word verification back: "Acknowledged."

Just as Cris steeled himself once again, firming

his resolve to stay cool — and cruel — until it was all over, the last five words of Traynor's communication came through and almost broke down the shield he had just constructed.

"Good hunting, folks. Hurry home."

Eight seconds before liftoff, the massive engines beneath the capsule roared to life. When the engines had built up sufficient thrust to get the missile off the ground, exploding bolts went off to release the clamps that held the rocket in place. In the same instant, the carefully camouflaged cover plate above the capsule swung open, revealing the early evening sky over North Dakota.

Almost imperceptibly at first, then with rapidly increasing speed, the missile rose out of the cylinder where it had resided for years. It was finally being used — not to kill other men, but to help save them.

For Cris, Tony, and Maura, the chase into space was under way.

25

April 29, 2036

That wasn't so bad, thought Cris as silence descended abruptly over the capsule. A lot of noise, a little shaking, and we're up.

"Sure we are," Tony said. "Better than the alternative, don't you think?" Cris realized that he had spoken his last few words instead of just thinking them.

"So that's what it's like to ride a rocket," he mused, ignoring Tony's question.

"More or less," Maura observed. "Don't forget, we're a lot less fragile than the people who have been in space before us."

She had a point. They didn't have to worry about the stress of multiple G-forces on their bodies as the missile made its ascent. Cris and the others had felt the pressure, but it did not greatly inhibit their ability to move since their "muscles" were many times stronger than those of human beings. And it had no effect at all on their ability to breathe, because they didn't need to breathe in the first place.

That was the biggest single difference, and the cyborgs' biggest advantage as astronauts over their human counterparts. Their life-support systems were built in, giving them even more survival security than a man in a space suit would have with none of the risks. Their "suits" couldn't be ripped or punctured — at least not very easily — and having no oxygen was no problem at all. Only their brains needed that sort of sustenance, and those organs were safely enclosed in artificial craniums that couldn't crack or leak. Cyborg Commandos were the ultimate astronauts; perhaps some day they would be used to journey to the stars. But right now, Cris and his comrades would settle for achieving orbit around Earth.

Just as it exhausted its fuel and detached from the capsule, the booster that had carried them some ninety miles aloft was able to get the capsule moving at orbital velocity. If the rocket had not done its job, the capsule would have simply traveled in a long parabola, rising to the fringe of the atmosphere and then plummeting down again, giving the occupants little, if any, choice over where — or how — they would come down.

In fact, the missile's engines stayed burning for

a few seconds after Cris stopped noticing the roar of the fuel exploding within them. But by then, they were effectively in the vacuum of outer space — a place where sound could not travel, because no air existed to serve as a medium of transmission. The CCs had switched from voice to radio communication just before liftoff, and would stay in touch electronically until they re-entered the atmosphere.

"My indicators are all green," said Tony, "which means either they're broken or we're in orbit. I figure we'll find out one way or the other in the next few minutes."

Cris trusted the equipment in the capsule and the men who had installed it, but nevertheless he was relieved and grateful a short time later, when it became obvious that they were falling *around* the planet beneath them instead of *toward* it.

"Okay, everybody," he said. "Let's get oriented."

"Give yourself a minute, Cris, and *look* at this," Maura said. "We may never get this chance again."

He had noticed the view before, of course, but hadn't taken the time or the effort to really appreciate it. "Just for a minute," he responded — and then, once he concentrated, he found it hard to tear his eyes away.

The panorama was breathtaking. Before him, the stark blackness of space contrasted with near-blinding sharpness against the gentle white of clouds and the pale blue of the Pacific Ocean. He turned to look through the viewport in front of the empty seat — John's seat — and noticed immediately how green and lush the forests of the northwest United States looked between the broken clouds of the late afternoon sky. From this distance, and in this small part of the world, he could see no evidence of the devastation that the invaders had wrought. "We're not through yet, you bastards," he muttered. "There's a lot of this world still worth saving, and we're going to do just that."

"That's tellin' 'em, pal," Tony said. "But you better speak up. I'm not sure this ugly dude in front of us heard you."

Could it be? Cris jerked his head around with such force that, if he hadn't been strapped in, his now-weightless body would have been catapulted out of his seat and into the nearest wall.

A few miles beneath them, rising in an arc that would carry it out over the waters of the Pacific, was a small, dark spot, easily visible even to normal sight against the backdrop of clouds.

"It might be another rocket," Maura said.

"We'll be able to tell the difference real soon," Cris responded. "And we won't fire until it gets above us anyway. Sit tight, guys. . . ."

Seconds later, there was no doubt in anyone's mind. The object leaving the planet at uncanny speed was certainly a teleborg — and a big one. The spot became a blob, a roughly circular disk at least a hundred and fifty yards in diameter with an irregular edge.

It was coming up almost vertically, on a path that would intersect with the capsule's orbit. The vessel would be ahead of it and moving away from it, but for a short span of time the two bodies would be mere miles apart. The CCs couldn't adjust the speed of their vessel, slowing down to keep the gap between them and their target from widening, or they would fall out of orbit prematurely. But out here, where visibility was flawless and obstructions were nonexistent, line of sight was virtually infinite. They could hit anything they could see — and they could see an object of this size for a long, long distance.

The teleborg either didn't notice the capsule or, more likely, was not paying it any heed; all that mattered to the thing was getting into the safety of outer space where it could safely recover from the beating it had just taken. As the creature passed through their orbital path, presenting its thin outer edge to his vision, Cris thought he could see tentacles and other protrusions coming out of its upper surface as the sun's rays caught the thing in profile. But the extremities were either hanging motionless or oscillating limply, seemingly not being controlled by the consciousness of which they were a part. All of its energy, at the moment, was being devoted to getting far away as fast as it could.

As the creature continued its ascent and rose higher than the orbit their capsule was following, the three cyborgs got their first look at a teleborg's weak spot. The underside of the thing was light-colored and practically featureless. Flames were shooting out of a ring of nozzles about half as large in diameter as the creature's body — flames that helped to make it an even more vulnerable target, against the utter blackness of space, than it would have been even if the rockets had not been firing.

The thing seemed to be making no efforts at evasion or course correction. "This is going to be almost too easy," Cris said as he extended his arms so that his knuckles protruded beyond the capsule wall. His computer-assisted aiming all but assured him of hitting his target even before he fired, and he almost wished there was a way he could disengage it to make the maneuver just a little challenging.

"But no less enjoyable," Tony quipped. "Here, let me give you a better angle. No sense being uncomfortable while you're having target practice." As he said that, Tony activated the small maneuvering jets on one side of the capsule, causing it to rotate slightly so that Cris's viewport was precisely lined up with the creature. It was now rapidly receding into the void above them, but Cris still had plenty of time. Nothing on Earth, native to the planet or otherwise, could outrun a laser beam.

"Do it!" Tony cried exultantly.

Beams of coherent light shot out of each of Cris's hands and traveled across the gap to the target in a fraction of a millisecond. The lasers cut off automatically a tenth of a second after Cris's mental order to fire, but that was time enough.

Almost instantaneously, the flames coming from the nozzles on the teleborg's underside were accompanied by two other noticeable bursts of light and fire — explosions where the beams had struck. Before anyone in the capsule could voice a reaction to that, their view of the creature's body was totally obscured by the biggest fireball Cris had ever seen. No sound reached their ears from the conflagration, of course, but they didn't need to hear the explosion to appreciate its power.

"Yahoo!" Tony shrieked.

"You did it!" Maura said.

But Cris wasn't accepting congratulations just yet. "Burn, you sucker! Burn!" he growled, keeping his eyes fixed on the globe of flame that burned like a miniature sun. He assumed that people on the ground could see it, even against a daytime sky, and he hoped they would know, or soon come to know, what it was.

Then the flames died out, almost as abruptly as they had come to life. Apparently all of the fuel the teleborg had been carrying had gone up at the same time. The fire couldn't survive without a supply of air, so after the fuel had been consumed in the initial blast the fireworks came to a quick end.

And so had the teleborg. All that remained in Cris's field of vision were chunks of matter, the sunlight catching each of them briefly as they flew in all directions outward from the origin of the explosion. Any of the pieces that fell back toward Earth would be incinerated by friction with the atmosphere on re-entry.

"One down," Cris said with grim satisfaction as he pulled his hands inside the capsule and leaned back in his seat.

"I want the next one," Maura said, rubbing her palms together gleefully.

"My pleasure," Cris said in acknowledgment. "It sure feels *good*. . . ."

. . . Bad! What was happening? The Master's most powerful, most unassailable servants were being destroyed! Unthinkable, yet undeniable — happening even as It watched, perplexed.

For the first time since Its forces descended on this planet, the Master began to examine, to question, what It had done. Was it possible that It had underestimated the resources and the determination of this insignificant race? It did not like being introduced to new feelings, new sensations. But another one was being born in Its consciousness:

Desperation.

26

April 29-30, 2036

In the next five hours, the chasers from Manitowoc made a little more than three circuits of the globe and personally accounted for the destruction of five more teleborgs. Everything went as they had expected, both the good and the bad.

"John should be here," Maura said sadly. "More than anyone else on Earth, he *deserves* to be here. He came so close . . ."

"He gave me a piece of advice a long time ago," said Cris, "that I've never forgotten. In the final analysis, it's not *how* you get the job done that matters — as long as you do it. I wish he was here too, but if he could talk to us right now I'm sure he wouldn't be feeling sorry for himself. He would be happy for us, and proud of us, because we're getting the job done. In fact, this is the best tribute to him that I can think of. We're doing it, we're succeeding, and if that can't bring him back, it can at least give his death some meaning."

"I'm ashamed of what I thought when I first heard about him," said Tony. "He was the best, wasn't he?"

"Yeah," said Cris. "Yeah, he was." Then a thought struck him, and he unstrapped himself from his seat and began to make his way carefully across the cabin.

"What . . . ?" Maura didn't immediately understand.

"One more tribute. This one's for John."

He strapped himself into the extra seat and locked his body into firing posture. About ten minutes later Cris blasted another teleborg, but this time no one spoke immediately afterward. After a moment of silence, Cris turned in the seat, brought the knuckles of his right hand to his mouth, and imitated blowing across them — the way John had always marked the end of a successful combat encounter. "I think," he said solemnly, "that's the way he would have done it."

To no one's surprise, the generator sputtered and died before they had gotten very far into their second orbit. Tony kept a close watch on their power from then on, and was able to estimate that between the charge stored up in the batteries and what they could get out of his leg unit, they could stay aloft safely for only four complete orbits. "We could go five," he said when that announcement met with moans of disappointment, "but in order to have enough power for re-entry, we'd have to go without heat for about half of that last orbit, and by the time I'd have to throw the switch to ignite the retro-rockets I might not be moving too fast."

"That's not much of a choice," Cris said.

"That is basically what I was trying to say," remarked Tony. "I figure about another half-hour before we start putting on the brakes."

They went out in a blaze of glory, encountering two teleborgs almost simultaneously. Cris and Maura split the duty, timing their laser blasts to go off at the same time, and two more miniature suns flared briefly into life, each adding another glimmer of brightness to the hopes of the human race.

"If everyone else is having as much success as we are," said Maura, "then this is a day these . . . creatures will regret ever having seen."

"And if everyone's as low on power as we are, this whole mission is going to come to an end very soon. At our present rate of power consumption, the meter says we'll run out of electricity before we finish re-entry. Cris, we have to start worrying about getting *down*." Tony's voice went from casual to anxious in the space of those two sentences, and the impact of his last few words was not lost on either Cris or Maura.

"I could rig up some wires to bleed power from our primary batteries," she suggested.

"Better not," Cris said. "We might need everything we've got to make it back to the base when we do come down."

"But we've gotta *get* back!" Tony was starting to panic, and Cris had to do something about that.

"Relax, relax," he said, stalling until he could think of something more encouraging or calming.

"We gotta be sure. We gotta turn off the heat," Tony said before Cris could continue.

That was it . . . the margin they needed! "No!" Cris said as the realization struck him. "We don't have to turn it off now, but we don't need to keep it on all the way down."

"The heat from re-entry—" Maura began.

Too excited to worry about being polite, Cris cut her off. "The readout on the power meter measures what we'll use if we keep the capsule heating coils on all the way down. But a few minutes after we contact the atmosphere again, this place is going to get very warm all by itself. . . ." He waited for Tony to jump in and finish that statement, and his friend — true to form — didn't disappoint.

". . . And we can turn off these power-hungry heaters!"

"Yep. Will that give you enough juice to jockey us down to a safe landing?"

"I'd bet my bottom on it!"

Maura chuckled and delivered a line that sent them all into gales of laughter. "S-24," she said with false solemnity, "you should never bet more than you can afford to lose."

Epilogue

The capsule carrying P-17, O-33, and S-24 returned to Earth about fifteen miles east and twenty miles south of Manitowoc — remarkably close to its intended splashdown point. It was a successful ending to a mission that, for all the hardship and tragedy woven through it, came off just as it had been planned.

Cris, Maura, and Tony thought they had done well, and they were right. But they were even more gratified when they discovered how successful "Chase Into Space" had been on a worldwide scale. That was the biggest piece of good news waiting for them when they got back to Manitowoc several hours after landing.

And there was other news, of course. . . .

Traynor had insisted on being the one to tell the three of them about Nora's death, and he made the initial blow as soft as it could have been. But it still hit hard.

Cris dealt with his grief silently at first, suppressing his sorrow and trying to concentrate on the good things about what had happened. She had died before John, so she was spared the pain of finding out about him. She would never again have to cope with the strain of worrying about the safety of her son and the others she had come to love. And finally, she was at peace, able to rest for the first time in years. Wherever she was now, she was better off.

All of this knowledge consoled Cris, and he took strength from the presence and sympathy of the people he loved. But later, when he was alone, Cris Holman wept harder and longer than ever before. And it was a long, long time before he got accustomed to not seeing his mother waiting for him when he returned from a mission.

* * *

"Chase Into Space" was a marvelous success in terms of actual results, with a side benefit that no one anticipated.

One hundred twenty-seven teleborgs around the world had been impregnated with super-rich nutrients. Of those, six were destroyed on the ground and nearly two-thirds of the ones that did try to escape were annihilated by the CCs who had gone into orbit. Cyborg Commando casualties were unbelievably light: one unit killed, two others damaged but able to get back to their bases under their own power. All of the CCs who had gone into orbit had returned safely to Earth. Every bit of that was extremely good news to Cris, Maura, and Tony . . . until each of them thought about who the "one unit killed" was.

A second set of launches took place a week later, and this time the "chasers" could only kill only about twenty percent of the teleborgs that were assaulted on the ground — because, to the ecstatic amazement of all concerned, most of the teleborgs that were bombed and strafed by conventional air forces did not take flight. Stubbornly, futilely, as if knowing the attempt to flee would do no good, they stayed entrenched where they were and fought to the death — their deaths.

It appeared as though the teleborgs had the ability to exchange information — or, more likely, that they were taking orders from some higher form of life. If that was the case, then that life form had made a big mistake. Now that the teleborgs had apparently been "brainwashed" into thinking that leaving the planet would be fatal to them, they were sitting ducks. They could be killed where they sat, either by air strikes or by well-coordinated ground assaults led by Cyborg Commando teams.

Thanks to what the original "chasers" had done, it was no longer necessary to send CCs into space in order to kill the rest of the teleborgs. Over the next few months, the forces of man methodically and efficiently did away with many of the creatures that had sat like festering sores on the face of their planet. Victory was by no means assured, but defeat was no longer just around the corner — and for all of mankind, that was very good news indeed.

* * *

The brain of former Cyborg Commando R-9 would never realize what it — he — had done for the world by managing to survive its installation back into the body of Jeff McDonnell. The young man would remain alternately catatonic and irrational until the day he died, but it was soon apparent that he would live for a long time. The work of Nora Whitaker, Francis Higgins, and others like them — and the sacrifice of Jeff McDonnell — was not in vain.

Other transplant reversals were attempted in the following weeks, all of them on CCs who were willing to take the chance or who, like Jeff McDonnell, were unable to make the choice for themselves. The successes outnumbered the failures practically from the start, and less than six months later transplant reversals were standard procedure — or, at least, as close as they would ever be to attaining that status.

Two happy results came out of that breakthrough. First, as had been anticipated, the ranks of the Cyborg Commando Force grew by leaps and bounds; thousands of people were quite willing to become CCs and help reclaim their planet, once they had the assurance that they'd be able to resume normal, human lives when the fighting was over.

Second, although overy one of them was given the chance to retire and regain their human forms, only a very small percentage of the original Cyborg Commandos took immediate advantage of the offer. Just knowing that the transplant could be reversed was good enough for them. Cris Holman's reaction was typical, and he spoke for Tony and Maura as well when ho said it: "The longer I stay the way I am, the sooner it will be until everyone can change back. Right now there's still work to be done, and I plan to keep this job until it becomes obsolete."

* * *

The Master had known rage before; these upstarts had angered It more than once. Before, Its fury had always been accompanied by arrogance and disdain. But now the anger was underscored by a different set of emotions: tension and anxiety, and an ever-increasing desperation.

It was beginning to know the feeling of an animal trapped in a corner from which there is no escape. It could not — would not — stop fighting. It

317

would not give up, because surrender was totally foreign to Its way of thinking. If all of Its forces were destined to die, then destiny would be served. But It would make sure that man's victory was an empty one.

For what point is there in saving a world if the world itself is destroyed in the process?

Authors' note

Players of the CYBORG COMMANDO™ Game will notice some minor differences between specific aspects of the game rules and the way those same aspects are described in this and the other CYBORG COMMANDO books.

These apparent discrepancies are intentional and not meant to cause any confusion or concern among game players. As in other cases where role-playing game environments have been "translated" into novelizations, it was deemed necessary by the authors to deviate somewhat from the strictures of the game for the sake of telling an entertaining story centered around the actions of a few major characters.

The story lines in the books are *based on* the same premise and the same background that serves as the foundation for the game — they are not directly *drawn from* the game rules. If all the readers of the books who are also players of the game can understand and appreciate this distinction, they will be able to enjoy both types of works to the fullest.